D0871561

BAD BOY

BAD BOY

Diana Wieler

**Delacorte
Press**

Published by
Delacorte Press
Bantam Doubleday Dell Publishing Group, Inc.
666 Fifth Avenue
New York, New York 10103

This book was originally published in Canada by Groundwood Books/
Douglas & McIntyre Ltd.

Library of Congress Cataloging in Publication Data

Wieler, Diana J.
    Bad boy / by Diana Wieler.
        p.   cm.
    Summary: A. J. Brandiosa becomes the bad boy of the Cyclones hockey
team, and learns that his best friend is gay, as he tries to cope with his own
sexuality during his senior year in high school.
    ISBN 0-385-30415-3
    [1. Hockey—Fiction.   2. Friendship—Fiction.   3. Homosexuality—
Fiction.]   I. Title.
PZ7.W6354Bad   1991
[Fic]—dc20   90-46676
                                                                     CIP
                                                                      AC

Book Design by Diane Stevenson/SNAP·HAUS GRAPHICS

Manufactured in the United States of America

March 1992

10   9   8   7   6   5   4   3   2   1

BVG

For my husband, Larry,
who relived his moments
of hockey glory for me,
over and over and over.

· ONE ·

THE MUSIC WAS blaring, a solid wall of sound that pressed A.J. Brandiosa against the wall. His shoes were vibrating; he counted at least thirty 200-pounders bouncing and bobbing under the orange lights. No wonder the floor shook. A.J. could envision the newspaper headlines: "Beer Barrel Polka Kills 100" or "Dancers Bring Down the House." It was enough to make him smile.

It had been a summer of weddings. There were 40,000 people in Moose Jaw, but it had never shrugged off the small-town feeling. Weddings were entertainment, a place for the old folks to whirl once again on the dance floor, a chance for the not-quite-nineteens to get over to the bar. It didn't matter if you knew the bride and groom or not. Once the buffet table was cleared, weddings were fair game for anyone wearing a tie. And nobody seemed to mind—"What the hell? My Lori's only gonna get married once, if we're lucky. Have a beer, kid."

A.J. crossed his arms over his chest and felt the fabric of

his dark suit stretch dangerously. The suit was only a year old, but he knew he could rip the seams if he tried. One quick tug, like touching his elbows together, and it would give. He was almost tempted to try.

At sixteen, A.J. was short and stocky, with wide palms and broad shoulders and muscled thighs that pushed against the seams of his suit pants. His dark hair curled when it grew too long, and for that reason he kept it short. It still curled, over his ears and behind his neck. "Like Pavarotti, so handsome!" his aunts cried.

They were faking it, of course, the Italian bit. A.J.'s family hadn't seen its home town of Caserta for eighty-five years, and his aunts only knew Pavarotti because they'd watched him on TV.

A.J. was watching a girl. He liked the way her brown hair curled in around her bare neck, and the way she threw her head back when she laughed. So what if her pink satin dress was stretched a little tight across her backside?

A.J. wasn't chunky anymore. Ten months of sweating it out with a second-hand weight set in his friend's basement had made the difference. But your mirror had its own memory. It knew where all the bumps used to be, and it would never let you forget it. A.J. was the last guy in the world who'd write somebody off over a little extra padding.

Others would, though. Pink Satin had been sitting with her girlfriends all night. None of them seemed to be dancing.

So come on, he kept telling himself. He must have taken a dozen deep breaths, getting ready to walk over, but somehow he was still standing against the wall, a half-glass of warm beer in his hand.

A.J. looked left and right. Where was Tully when you needed him? His friend was so good at this kind of thing, introducing himself and breaking the ice. He didn't agonize over it or use stupid lines; he didn't come on like a jock. He just pulled up a chair and started talking. Pretty soon the girls would be laughing, then dancing, and A.J. would slide along, caught up in the current of the night.

Except it wasn't happening. The boy stared sullenly at the dance floor. The polka had melted into Dean Martin. Dean Martin, for Pete's sake. Why did he come to these things?

Something slammed into his right side, and his drink shot out of the glass and onto the carpet. A.J. whirled around, cursing. It was Tully. The bump had been a friendly hip check.

"You shouldn't jump me like that." Tully grinned. "You know I can't see a thing with these dark glasses." He pulled them out of his pocket and held them up.

Tulsa Brown was an illusion. He was taller than A.J., and from a distance he looked lean. But A.J. knew where the muscles were; he knew the time Tully had put in on the weight bench. When they were in junior high, A.J. could outwrestle his friend every time. It had been a game. A.J. was still fifteen pounds heavier, but it didn't seem to matter anymore. When they went at it now, A.J. found himself grappling for an advantage. If he let down his guard for a moment, wham! Tully would take him down.

Tonight Tully was flying. His suit jacket had disappeared, and his rumpled sleeves were up over his elbows. He'd wrapped his tie around his forehead like a headband, and his cedar-gold hair stuck out at crazy angles. He looked just like himself.

A.J. waved his hand in front of his nose. "Jeez, Tul. What's your cologne? Eau du Miller Lite?"

Tully beamed. "So I'm sloppy."

"And you're getting sloppier, every beer. Hold off a bit, hey? Don't forget—we're in training."

"Right. Three more polkas and home we go. I can hardly handle the excitement."

Tully was cheering him up, as usual. A.J. felt light-headed and silly and a little braver. He glanced over at Pink Satin. "Go tell the DJ to pick up the pace about twenty years, Tul. Something we can dance to."

Tully's eyes lit up. "Hey, I'm game if you are." He put his hand on A.J.'s shoulder. "But you know, people will talk."

"Jesus!" A.J. pulled back, flushing crimson. But his friend was laughing, and it drew him in. "You goof." A.J. grinned sheepishly. He jerked his head towards Pink Satin's table. "Those two."

Tully studied the girls. "Lucky kids. They're just begging for it, I can tell by their eyes. Well, let's not let them suffer any longer." He started across the room towards the disc jockey's table, stumbling just once.

It worked. As the last refrain of "Tiny Bubbles" was fading, the sound system burst into a fifties rock classic. Hope shot up inside A.J. like a geyser. This was perfect, just perfect! Pink Satin and her friend were looking wistfully at the dance floor as it filled with the under-thirty crowd.

A.J. fidgeted in beat with the music. He saw his friend weaving his way back through the crowd and gestured at him to hurry.

"Come on, come on," he muttered under his breath. Just then, a hand clamped around his arm.

"A.J.! How's things? How's your father? Look at you, I can't believe how you've grown!"

A.J. felt the night swirl and sink. "Uh, hi, Auntie Marie."

She was short and stout with cheeks that burned bright with rouge. "I saw your name in the paper. Famous! I cut it out for my scrapbook. What's it all about, anyway?"

"Hockey, Auntie Marie. I made the Cyclones, Triple A." He knew she had no idea of what that meant. "They publish the names of all the teams' players."

She wasn't listening. Still clutching A.J.'s arm, she leaned across him and hollered at a nearby table.

"Mike. Mike! It's A.J., can you believe it? Come say hello."

Miserably A.J. looked over at Tully, who had shown up at last and was killing time by playing air guitar. Rocking and writhing, he was in a world of his own, with the music and an imaginary guitar.

A.J. managed to catch his friend's attention, and rolled his eyes. Tully winked. Relatives were a hazard of any wedding.

Then Uncle Mike's cigar breath assaulted him. "So you're a hotshot hockey player now. Good for you. Our family's as good as anybody. We'll show those bastards, eh?"

A.J. felt queasy, as if he had been caught in a lie. It was true, he was on the Cyclones' roster. He was listed as a defenseman in the newspaper article Marie had clipped and saved. But the newspaper had printed the facts, not the story.

This wasn't A.J.'s first shot at the Cyclones. The year before, he and Tully had both signed up for the five-day tryouts. Tully made it to day three; A.J. was cut almost instantly.

It had stunned him. For almost seven years A.J. had played defense, and he thought he played it pretty well. He'd had no trouble getting on community club teams. Coaches started calling him in late summer. But playing for Riverside or Eastend—that was bulldozer hockey. The Cyclones were Triple A and Triple A was just below Junior, and that was something else altogether.

Tully had shrugged it off. "Your loss, guys!" he'd cried, thumbing his nose at the arena. To A.J. he had said, "Well, that's genetics for you. We just didn't get our share of the Triple A chromosomes."

But A.J. couldn't kid about it. The thought that he'd underestimated the competition, or worse, overrated himself, smouldered inside him.

"We didn't train hard enough," he said when he could finally talk about it. "We didn't try hard enough."

In October he'd started running windsprints. A.J. hated running, he was plagued by side cramps, but he knew it would build up his lung capacity. Just before Christmas, he'd bought a second-hand weight set that seemed to fit better in Tully's basement than his own. The first few nights he'd stumbled home like an arthritic gorilla, unable to straighten his arms.

"Take it easy," Tully had kidded. "The Olympics aren't for another four years."

"I've got focus," A.J. had said.

"You've got *tunnel vision.*" But within a week Tully was

doing arm curls while A.J. was on the bench. He took to it so naturally—the squats, the leg lifts, the rowing—that A.J. shook his head. He despised "natural athletes," but no one could hate Tully.

That winter they played for a decent club team, Tully as a winger and A.J. on defense. Most other evenings they spent in Tully's basement, puffing until their T-shirts swam and the windows steamed.

Sometimes Tully's sister, Summer, crept down the basement stairs, sitting so quietly that they didn't notice her at first. Summer was fourteen then, but somehow smarter and sharper than A.J. could remember being at fourteen. She was small but well-rounded. Her behind reminded A.J. of a pert upside-down heart. She had burnt-gold, almost brown hair, and a mouth that could puncture from fifteen paces.

"It stinks in here," Summer would say suddenly. "And you're both a dripping, sweaty mess. I didn't know the infantile pursuit of machismo could be so utterly disgusting."

A.J. would blush, as much over "machismo" as "dripping, sweaty mess," but Tully would drop what he was doing.

"My darling baby sister," he would say, smiling wickedly. "Come give your brother a big hug."

Summer would shriek and bolt up the stairs. Tully would tear after her, trying to wrap his sweaty body around her. Resting on the bench, A.J. would reach for a towel and self-consciously wipe himself down. She made him feel awkward, whether she noticed him or ignored him. But he was infinitely glad the weight set was in Tully's house.

Tryouts for the Cyclones began at the end of August. The grueling workouts seemed easier this time. A.J. found he could slide from a skating drill to ice push-ups without too much trouble. But he wasn't as confident as the year before; he wasn't as anxious to put himself on display. Weight training wouldn't make him a better skater; wind-sprints wouldn't improve his passing. And he knew he had a few bad habits.

A.J. had the tendency to watch the puck on his stick, afraid he would lose it. "Get your head up, Brandiosa!" Coach Landau called, again and again. A.J. tried, but the minute the pressure was on, the moment he stopped think-ing about it, he slid back to his old way. In a scrimmage on day three, he was slammed into the boards by a vicious shoulder check he never saw.

A.J. dropped, the wind knocked out of him. He was on the ice a full minute, struggling with the pain and embar-rassment. Defensemen were supposed to dish it out, not take it.

Coach Landau skated over, full of concern, but as soon as he saw A.J. was all right, he glared at him.

"There are honest mistakes and there are dumb mistakes, Brandiosa. You can guess which kind that was."

A.J. staggered to his feet, sick with himself. That's it, he thought. He'd be gone at the end of the day. Damn it. Damn it all to hell.

But by some miracle he wasn't cut, and once he got over the surprise, he threw himself into practice on days four and five. The final roster was posted on a Friday and A.J. sidled up to it cautiously. He tried to set his face so that whatever happened, it wouldn't show.

When he saw his name, he read it three times, numb. The next minute Tully was pounding him on the back.

"Holy mother, aren't we something! This team is going to the finals at last. They finally got us, the lucky dogs!"

Tully's jubilance spilled over, and A.J. was suddenly awash with it. He felt his guts uncurling. The horrible week was over and they were on—he was on. He couldn't help the stupid grin that cracked his stony mask. He was high.

A.J. was on the verge of whooping it up with the rest of them, when he saw Landau heading over, his arms full of equipment. The coach paused near the cluster of boys.

"Glad to see this enthusiasm," Landau said dryly, "but remember, I've got another list. There are a dozen guys who are waiting for one of you to slide. You've got to keep your heads up." He looked at A.J.

By the time you hit Triple A, the guys said, you couldn't kid yourself. You knew what kind of player you were. A.J. knew. But in case he didn't, Coach Landau's eyes were telling him now.

Marginal. The word seemed to rattle in A.J.'s head like a ball bearing, even though no one had said it.

That afternoon he took home his new jersey, number 27, rolled up with his equipment in his duffel bag. And he took home the word, wondering how he was ever going to shrug it off.

Now Uncle Mike was driving him crazy. He had a drink in one hand and A.J.'s lapel in the other, and for over an hour he'd been pounding the facts of life into the boy's brain. It was profound information, things like "You wanna eat—you gotta work" and "Don't ever go into the landscaping business. You'll ruin your back."

A.J. was bored and irritable. It was getting close to midnight and the party was deteriorating. From the corner of his eye, he saw Pink Satin get up and leave.

He shifted tiredly and let out a deep, disgusted breath. Why did old people ignore you most of the time, but become determined to "shape your life" the moment you had something better to do?

"Guidance," Uncle Mike was saying. "Young people don't have no guidance. That's why they're screwing up—drugs and crap."

So where were you, A.J. thought. Where were you and everybody else at Christmas when Dad and I made a turkey—a $25 turkey, for Pete's sake—and nobody had the guts to show up.

"Don't get me wrong." Uncle Mike dug his finger into A.J.'s chest. "It's the parents' fault. Don't have no discipline themselves, never mind the kids. Out till every hour of the goldang night, do whatever the hell they please. No respect for home and family."

A.J. felt the words snag, like a fishhook on an underwater branch. Back up, he thought. Make an excuse to get away.

"We been married twenty-seven years, Marie and I," Uncle Mike continued, "and do you think it's been easy? Do you? Do you? Hell, no!" Uncle Mike almost toppled over. "But I stuck by her and she stuck by me, the way it says in the Bible."

A.J.'s stomach was on fire. He could hear all the warning signals in his head; he knew these sounds. Go, he ordered himself. Go now.

But the old man had draped a conspiratorial arm around the boy's shoulders and was leaning on him heavily. His fetid smell—sweat and smoke and rum—was all around A.J., pinning him.

"Listen to me, A.J. All cats are gray in the dark. It's family that counts. Promise me something, hey? When you get married, you'll do right by us. A good girl, not like, you know . . . the wrong kind. Promise me . . ."

"Shut up."

". . . you won't go screwing around where everybody can see . . ."

"Shut up!" A.J.'s arm shot out, a reflex. He didn't even feel the pressure of contact, but Uncle Mike staggered back, banging into a pillar. His drink tumbled to the carpet.

A.J. could envision himself grabbing the old man's shoulders and slamming him against the pillar. He could see it and he wanted it, and it scared him. He took a step backwards.

"You're drunk, Mike," he said, his voice barely audible. "Go home and sleep it off."

Uncle Mike stared back, his eyes bulging. A.J. turned and pushed his way through the crowd, heart pounding, cheeks burning.

He kept going until he was out of the dark dance hall and in the hotel lobby. The bright lights made him dizzy. He sat down on a couch between the pay phones and the front desk.

What was that, A.J.? he asked himself. He's almost sixty years old. You didn't have to push him. All right, so he's obnoxious. He's always been obnoxious. You've put up with it for sixteen years. What the hell was that?

But he knew. He had lost control, and it was still lost. His insides were shaking.

Why did everybody have to have a theory? How come a divorce couldn't just belong to the people who'd had the marriage? Alina Brandiosa had been gone four years.

"Hey," said the clerk at the front desk. "Hey, you. Are you sick or something? Do you want me to call a cab?" She looked nervous. "We just had the rugs done, you know?"

A.J. jerked himself to his feet, before she called hotel security. The night was pressing too hard on him.

"Why don't you eat your rugs, lady," he muttered, walking back towards the dance hall.

It was time to go home, or at least time to go. He pictured driving around with Tully with the windows open. It was cold for September, but A.J. didn't care. He wanted to hang his arm out the window and let the air blast his face. Maybe they could drive to Regina. A.J. quickened his step.

Tully owned a red 1969 Mustang, almost original and almost perfect. It had been his parents' car, the one they drove around the country when they were hippies, traveling to rock concerts and just bumming around. Tully thought he'd been conceived in that car. "It was the state of Oklahoma. You can guess which city," he said with a grin.

Mr. and Mrs. Brown were respectable now. Tully's mother ran a health food store and his father was a counselor for the handicapped. They bought a station wagon and lent the car to Tully on the condition that he love it and cherish it forever.

A.J. loved the Mustang. It was a notchback—the kind

with a boxy roof—a classic if there ever was one. The engine was a 289 V8, not racing power by any means, but enough. A.J. loved the vibration of it, the rhythmic way it idled and charged. He loved the white interior that still smelled faintly of leather and wrapped him up, safe. It was a quiet car. Even gunning down the highway with the stereo pounding, the Mustang felt as private as a bedroom. You could talk in there.

A.J. wasn't good at talking. He could answer questions all right, and if somebody wanted to joke around and trade insults, he could do that, too. But telling was hard. It took him a long time to get started.

Tully knew that. "Let's drive to Junior's for a shake," he would say. Junior's was a tiny burger place in Regina, almost 45 miles away. It was an hour's leisurely drive, each way. That was usually long enough.

Tully could be a whirlwind in a car, driving, talking, eating and powercramming for a test, all at the same time. But when he listened, that's all he did. He didn't interrupt, he didn't give advice.

A.J., staring out the windshield at the passing prairie, could feel himself unwinding as he talked. He never solved anything, but it helped him to go home when sometimes he didn't think he could. The passenger seat of the Mustang was a little cubicle of air where he could say what he thought, without thinking. He loved that car.

And right now he was in the mood for one of Junior's shakes. A.J. eagerly pushed open the door to the dance hall. But Tully was gone.

· TWO ·

Dawn cut a broad arc against the retreating violet sky as the red Mustang rolled up in front of A.J.'s house. Tully turned off the engine and stepped out. The cold air was a rude surprise. He hunched his shoulders, conscious of his open collar and naked neck.

He felt grimy—the rumpled, chafed feeling of having slept in his clothes, although he hadn't slept at all. Last night's liquor was a bitter film in his mouth now, and there was a dull, buzzing pain the size of a dime behind each eye. More than anything, he wanted to get back in his car, go home and collapse into bed. It was still early enough for his parents and his siren of a sister to be asleep.

They'd never know, Tully told himself. You could get out of this one with your skin.

But he had hockey practice this morning, and there was no question about missing it. He couldn't even be late. In Triple A the coach didn't chew you out, he locked the door.

This year had been an awakening. He and A.J. had only been to a few practices, but already Tully could tell that playing for the Cyclones wasn't going to be like playing for Riverside, or Eastend. The rules were the same—don't mouth off, don't be late, do what you're told—but they seemed different because Coach Landau enforced them. There was more barking, more goading, less horseplay and wildness. The parts Tully liked best were the parts that were disappearing.

"Well, why do you keep doing it?" Summer had asked once, in the blank way that sisters ask things like that. Tully had stared at her. Because it's like flying, was all he could think. There was prestige to making a team, and winning—especially scoring—was an incredible rush. But hurtling ahead under his own power, faster than he could run, faster even than he thought he could skate, was as close to the sky as he could get. Driving wasn't like that, and dancing wasn't like that. Nothing was like that.

Tully pushed himself away from the Mustang and headed for the house.

When there was no answer at the front door, he felt the prick of panic. What was taking so long? He knew Mr. Brandiosa wouldn't be home—he was on the early shift at the dairy—but A.J. always waited. He wouldn't just leave without me, Tully thought. Irritated, he jogged around to the back and peered through the window in the door.

He could see A.J.'s equipment laid out, arranged as carefully as a store display. The jersey was clean and supple, the stick bright with fresh tape. The pads—always foul things, gray and stiff because they couldn't be washed—were spaced in a half-circle, airing out.

Tully had seen this before but it still staggered him.

Nobody does this, he thought. His own gear was in the trunk of his car from last practice, fused by sweat into a solid mass that would make his eyes water when he opened his bag. But all the guys were like that. When you played hockey you were rumpled and rank. It didn't matter.

Except that the spread on the kitchen floor reminded him that for this guy, everything mattered. Tully tried the door, and finding it unlocked, gently pushed his way in.

It took three calls before A.J. sat upright, swearing. "All right, all right! I'm awake. Jesus."

"Good, I thought you were in a coma," Tully said, grinning. He was rooting around in a dresser drawer. In a moment he sent a pair of blue jeans sailing across the room; they landed on A.J.'s lap with a whump.

"Gotta forget the Wheaties today." Tully tossed a shirt onto the bed. "It's already ten after."

A.J. was sitting like a statue, his dark eyes fixed on his friend. Tully remembered that he was wearing last night's dress clothes, which looked like they had been wadded by a hydraulic press. He couldn't walk into the locker room like this. He turned and began rifling the dresser again.

"Mind if I borrow something?" he asked. There was still no response. Behind his back, Tully heard the rustle of sheets and then the sound of A.J. leaving the room for the bathroom down the hall.

What was the matter now? Tully wondered as he pulled on sweatpants and a rugby shirt. Was A.J. fighting with his dad again? Was he still strung out about how well he'd do on the team? Tully worried about him sometimes. What might look like a bad mood on somebody else could mean disaster for A.J. He was a guy who dissolved from the inside out.

The blond boy leaned out of the room. "Come on, superstar—quarter after!" he called down the hallway. It was enough to send them both barreling down the stairs. Tully revved up the car while A.J. gathered his gear.

The first few minutes of the drive were uncomfortably quiet.

"So, last night was a blast, wasn't it?" Tully asked.

"No," A.J. said abruptly.

Tully was taken aback. It had been a great night for him.

"What happened? You get roped by your relatives? Or did the floor open up and swallow all the girls?"

"No. It was the long walk home."

The words hit Tully in the chest. His memory clunked forward. The hotel was on the other side of the city.

He'd left the reception last night on a rush of adrenaline, blind to everything except where he was going. When he'd thought of A.J., briefly and much later, he'd assumed he'd caught a ride or something.

Or something. It would have been a long, long walk in sneakers; in dress shoes it had to be hell. No wonder A.J. was ticked off.

Still, he hadn't actually *promised* to drive A.J. home. And wasn't the whole point of going out to get some excitement? Adults were always saying you were supposed to grab every opportunity.

Except Tully knew he had a hair trigger when it came to opportunities. And he didn't so much take them as plunge into them. Head first. And sometimes he hit the bottom of the pool.

"Sorry," he said, his eyes on the road in front of him.

He had the feeling it was the first of many sorrys he'd have to say that day.

A.J. shrugged. "Yeah, well," he said. There was a pause, then, "You going to catch hell for not getting home?"

Tully welcomed the change of direction. "Supremely," he said.

"Was it worth it?"

Tully looked at him and winked. A.J. shook his head, grinning in spite of himself. Moments later the Mustang roared into the arena parking lot. The boys scrambled into the dressing room, flinging clothes, and made it onto the ice just in time. Coach Landau glared at them, then blew a short blast on his whistle.

A.J. had heard that Gary Landau had played in the NHL once, for about a year. He was a wiry man in his midthirties, with just a trace of stomach over his belt. His hair was solidly brown, the color of an acorn, but around his intent eyes there were lines where the wrinkles would be soon. Waiting on the ice, A.J. avoided those eyes. He was never quite sure what was behind them.

"All right, gentlemen," Landau called, "you get to play with your pucks today." Ripple of laughter. "But let's get you good and warm first. Give me five minutes of manmakers—right now!"

Manmakers—which A.J. thought was the stupidest name in the world—was a power skating drill. It was designed to build up your legs and lungs, and make you hate God for giving you legs and lungs in the first place. Starting at the backboards, the skaters sped to the blue line, stopped on a dime, then raced back to the boards. Next time it was the center line and back, then the farthest blue line.

The boys began, stiff-legged, grumbling a bit. Endurance skating was grueling, and everyone was inclined to back off, now that the team had been picked.

A.J. knew he couldn't back off. He was carrying the word with him; he felt it was stitched on his jersey. Number 27—marginal. It burned him, even now. He'd had another call this week, the coach from Riverside Community Club, asking him to play. He'd cut the call short, too short to be polite. He knew how easy it would be to slide back down to that kind of hockey. Just for a minute, though, he'd wished Landau had known somebody else wanted him.

Except he doesn't know, A.J. thought, charging for the blue line. And he won't. All that counts is here. He pushed the fury into his legs, elbowing out past the crowd.

He couldn't keep it up. At the three-minute mark he was gulping air, and the pain was like a small dagger in his side. A.J. was fast, good for short bursts over the ice, but he was too bulky to maintain it. He plowed forward, cursing himself, but he knew he was losing it.

"Drop!" Coach Landau cried suddenly. The boys skidded to a halt and fell to the ice where they were. A.J. went down so fast his helmet struck the ice. A "drop" command meant twenty push-ups.

For a few moments A.J. lay still, his nose an inch from the ice, his breath burning his face. Around him he heard wheezing, then the rustle of clothing and stifled moans as the boys began pushing their exhausted bodies up.

Listening to them, he almost grinned. This was one drill where weight training did help, where the endless lifts and curls made a difference. He took two deep breaths and dug his skate points into the ice to anchor himself. Body rigid, he pushed himself up lightly, easily.

"One, two, three," he muttered softly. He felt pressure in his shoulders, a stretching, but there was no pain. Out of the corner of his eye he saw the others slowing down, and he managed to quicken his pace. The exhilaration surged through him like liquid heat. He hoped Landau was watching. "Eleven, twelve, thirteen . . ."

When he had counted twenty, he forced himself up so fast he saw stars. He started circling unsteadily, proud he was the first one on his feet. He glanced in Landau's direction. The coach was busy setting out pylons, looking the other way. A.J. almost moaned out loud.

The orange pylons were spaced in an obstacle course, for puck control drills. One at a time, the boys were to thread their way in and around, carrying the puck.

The pylons made A.J. nervous. He was a charger, best in a straight line of attack. He could maneuver when he had to, but on a course like this he knew he was slow. He felt like a bear on a skateboard. And then there was the other thing: his eyes were drawn to the puck even before he started.

He got caught, once. Landau's cry of "Get it up, Brandiosa!" caused a chorus of guffaws. A.J. glared at the far boards, turning crimson under his helmet and visor. But he made it through his turn without any other mistakes, and slid gratefully back into the lineup.

Catching his breath, A.J. watched the others intently. Most were pretty good, but there were a few who looked awkward on this particular drill. A.J. was relieved that Landau was just as tough on them.

"Watch me, Millyard—not your pecker."

"Come on, come on! What kind of drugs are you on, Rudachuk?"

When it was Tully's turn, A.J. realized he'd forgotten all about his friend. There was no doubt Tully was exhausted. His skate blades hardly seemed to leave the ice as he moved towards the pylons.

He's been awake twenty-four hours, A.J. thought, wincing. How was Tully going to get through this?

But when the blond boy had the puck on his stick and leaned into the first curve, the tiredness fell away like a cloak. He wasn't fast, but he moved in and around the pylons with uncanny pacing. Back and forth, back and forth, like a metronome.

The group was silent now, and A.J. felt his own eyes growing wider. He knew his friend was a good skater, but he couldn't remember him being this good. He made the difficult loops look so effortless. It was eerie.

A.J. wasn't the only one who noticed. As Tully rounded the last curve, Landau said quietly, "Once more, Mr. Brown."

Tully turned and threaded his way through again, with the same easy grace. The puck never seemed to leave his stick. It wasn't spectacular, because drills never were spectacular, but it was surprising. Tully hadn't come onto the Cyclones as a hotshot.

When he came off the run, he bowed.

Some guys laughed, some groaned. A.J. grinned. That ham, he thought, feeling a small tug of envy.

Practice was almost over and everyone was tired and anxious to get into the shower. Sweat was on A.J. like a second skin. He felt dirty and defeated.

"All right," Landau said grimly, "we'll save the scrimmage for next time. I wouldn't put this bunch against a team of mother-in-laws. We'll finish up with some two-on-ones, *if* you don't mind," he added over the rumble of protest.

Two-on-ones were exactly what they sounded like. Two forwards, a winger and a center, advanced on a defenseman, trying to get around him to take a shot. It was practice for the forwards, and the goalie, of course, but the real pressure was on the defenseman, the man in the middle.

Tired as he was, A.J.'s heart began to pound as he waited his turn against the boards. He'd played against the winger, Al Weitzammer, before, on other teams. He's still got it, A.J. thought as he watched Weitzammer skillfully maneuver and fake his way to a shot every time. A.J. was out on the ice almost before Landau motioned at him.

The trio started at the center line, with A.J. positioning himself between the forwards and the goal. He was a good backwards skater and it served him well. He felt the winger going wide and echoed him effortlessly, forcing him wider. The seconds stretched painfully as Weitzammer hung back. When they were hardly ten feet from the goal crease, it happened. The winger suddenly slid in close, hardly a blur in A.J.'s right eye. He felt the pass fly behind him, but the second Weitzammer dropped his head, A.J. was there, connecting with a solid shoulder. The puck went skidding out against the boards.

A.J. stared into the mirror, letting his eyes slide out of focus until his face was a blur and the razor was only a glint in his hand. He was afraid to look at himself, afraid he'd break out laughing.

"Now *that's* defense! Good play, Brandiosa! Did everybody see that?"

It was no big deal, really. He'd always been good at anticipating shots. Hadn't every coach said that to him?

Except this time it felt different. After being tense for so long, he was swamped with relief, and it made him giddy. It was only one play, but it went a long way.

He couldn't show it, though. Triple A was cool hockey. A.J. scowled slightly as he drew the razor through the foam. But his teeth were laughing.

Tully sidled up to the sink next to him and casually turned on the taps. He soaked his face and neck with warm water, then leaned forward on his elbows, grinning at A.J.'s somber reflection.

"Hey, bigshot. Don't forget. I knew you when you were nobody."

A.J. coughed, choking back the crazy giggle that was sitting in his throat. But it was no good. He had to let go, or explode.

A.J. scooped up a handful of wet foam from the sink and let it fly. Splat! It caught Tully across the side of his head, over his ear. The blond boy whirled around, groping for a towel and swearing revenge.

"Foam fight!" somebody cried in the background.

"Gillette wars!"

Tully grabbed a can of shaving foam and dove for A.J., who had the good sense to run. He still got it—a white trail down his naked back. Sputtering with laughter, A.J. dodged around the lockers and darted for the sinks again. He needed ammunition.

There was a stray can on the counter. A.J. grabbed it and spun around, pressing hard on the button.

Splurrt.

"Oh, no—gel!" The spectators roared.

Tully smiled wickedly, advancing forward with his arm outstretched, spray can poised. Desperate, A.J. turned on the cold water tap full blast, positioning his palm under the spigot. The water shot across the room in a tight, icy stream, blasting Tully's left side. He yowled with surprise and twisted out of the way. A.J. giggled and took aim again.

"Well, well. Tulsa Brown."

The voice was low but surprisingly sharp. It cut through the giddy air like a saber.

Landau! A.J.'s heart skipped a beat and in one deft movement he'd silenced the tap. He straightened up apprehensively and looked over his shoulder, but Coach Landau wasn't there. It was only a guy, a player, one of them.

Just a panic attack, A.J. breathed. But as the moment stretched out and nobody moved, he felt his muscles tighten. What was this? Who was this guy? Why was he just standing there, staring at Tully?

The young man was tall, almost five-ten, A.J. guessed, and he was fresh out of the shower. His mahogany hair glinted red under the lights. He was wearing blue jeans, but his chest and feet were bare, and he'd slung his jersey over his shoulder. The number was twisted but readable: 19.

Number 19 was handsome in a hard-edged way, but unremarkable. Except for his eyes. They were a color A.J. had never seen before, a dark cement gray. And they were fastened on Tully like thumbtacks.

A.J. felt his stomach wrench. In his mind's eye he saw Tully hamming it up around the pylons—bowing, for Pete's sake. Now you've done it, you stupid ass, he thought bitterly. Old team members were wary of newcomers, even newcomers with talent.

A.J.'s heart was thumping in his ears. You weren't supposed to interfere. But you didn't let a friend take a beating. A.J.'s hands curled into fists.

But Number 19 didn't move. He stood maddeningly still, his mouth twisted in a faint smirk. A.J. glanced at Tully. His friend had pulled himself up tall, but the color had drained from his face. He still held the spray can, clutched in a death grip at his side.

What was this? What was going on? Number 19 was tall, but not that big, and Tully could scrap when he had to. Everybody was staring, for Pete's sake. Why didn't Tully just walk away or throw the first punch or something?

It was Number 19 who moved first. He stepped forward at last, brushing past Tully so slowly he could have been under water.

"Fancy feet, Tulsa," the boy whispered, the words as soft and insidious as a hypodermic needle. A.J. watched the bare shoulders slide easily into the crowd and disappear.

There was a second's pause, then somebody spoke. In a few moments, guys were milling around again, getting dressed. But their voices were subdued; the lighthearted mood had sunk.

A.J. was trying to sort out the images when Tully stepped past him and up to the sinks. The words were out before A.J. could stop them.

"Friend of yours?" he asked.

Tully turned away abruptly, as if he hadn't heard. He began walking towards the lockers. A.J. stared as if he'd been hit. He didn't notice that the foam on his back had melted, and was sliding into his shorts.

· THREE ·

IT WAS A long ride home. Tully was driving like a zombie, careening in and around the other cars, tromping on the gas. A.J. slouched in his seat, staring out the window to hide the way his heart lurched every time Tully cut somebody off or flew through an amber light. There were rules to being sixteen and male. One of them was that you never told a friend how to drive his car.

A.J. concentrated on the view out his window instead. On the sidewalk, early shoppers were fighting the cold wind that had caught September by surprise. The trees in the park were still green, pugnaciously clinging to summer, but there was no doubt. Autumn was in the clouds and in the wind. You could smell it, A.J. thought.

He felt the car sliding slowly, surreptitiously into the next lane, and he caught his breath. A horn blared and Tully swerved, jerking the Mustang back on course. The green half-ton they'd almost hit surged ahead. Its driver glared at them. A.J. chewed on the inside of his cheek.

Questions were crawling around inside him like ants, but he let them crawl. Tully never pressured him when something was wrong. He let A.J. unwind at his own speed. He'll tell me when he's ready, the boy thought.

Tully wasn't ready.

The Mustang pulled up in front of A.J.'s house and the boy hauled his equipment out of the back seat. Then he hesitated, leaning against the open door.

"You wanna come in—grab something to eat?" he asked. Then he shrugged. "Cartoons are still on."

Tully smiled ruefully, the first expression he'd been capable of in half an hour.

"Nah. I might as well face the firing squad now. Get it over with."

A.J. shouldered his duffel bag. "Maybe tonight, hey? We'll do some lifting or something?"

"Better call first. I might be busy attending my own funeral."

"Right." A.J. felt himself stalling. He shut the car door with a determined thud. "See you."

Tully waved and popped the clutch into second gear. A.J. paused in the driveway, watching the car gun down the quiet street.

Tully drove until he was out of sight, then pulled into the parking lot of a tiny strip mall. He switched off the ignition and sat, still buckled in his seat belt. He felt too exhausted to move. Just getting from the rink to here had been an ordeal.

He was frightened, and furious with himself. He'd frozen there in the locker room. If he could have laughed it off or walked away, it would have been nothing. Nobody would have noticed. But he'd stood there, pinned like a scared kid, and it had turned into an event. Even now he could feel the crowd's eyes on him, and A.J.'s bewildered stare.

It had begun last night. When he'd left the reception he'd gone to a party he'd heard was happening. He hardly knew anyone there but that wasn't a problem. Most were drunk and all were friendly. Tully didn't feel tired until early morning, and then he'd wandered into the backyard, thinking of catching a short snooze in his car.

But by the gate he met someone coming in, someone he did know, very well. Tully discovered he wasn't tired anymore and besides, the yard was dark and empty. There were three very nice minutes, three minutes that made his heart bang like a drum in his head and his throat, before he opened his eyes and looked over the shoulder and saw the fiery red dot burning a hole in the night.

It was a cigarette, and someone was smoking it. It was then that Tully realized the yard wasn't dark enough. Light washed out from the windows and the open door. There was enough light to make out a body and a face, and it worked both ways.

He was in his car and gone in a matter of seconds. But he'd had too good a summer and too much to drink to be afraid. He let the anxiety slide away.

In the locker room it had boomeranged back at him. Tully ran his hand across his eyes. It was the same face, he knew it. You didn't forget cheekbones like that, so high and sharp they seemed to be made of something harder than bone. And there was no mistaking the message in Number 19's shark-gray eyes:

All I've got to do is say the magic words, and you're out, ready or not. . . .

Tully's heart was pounding, even now. He wasn't ready, damn it. He was scared and he wasn't ready.

He knew the day was coming, and a small part of him was relieved. When you build a house of cards you know it'll come tumbling down sometime. But he was used to being liked. He had dates when he wanted them. When he told a joke, everybody laughed. When he drove up to school in the Mustang, there was an immediate cluster of guys leaning against the doors and fenders, willing to sit and shoot the breeze. And he had one good friend.

He wasn't ready to lose any of it.

So fix it, Tulsa, he told himself, and smarten up. Summer was over and school was back and he had to slide into the acceptable rut. Tully thought over the possibilities. There was a girl who sat in front of him in English, a pretty girl with nutmeg hair that fell in crinkles over her chair and swept across his desk when she leaned back to whisper to him. The hair intrigued him. Each long strand was so perfectly curled, yet separate from the others. He'd found himself wanting to touch it. Andrea. Andrea Knutson. She was nice, Tully thought. She would do.

But he had to fix the other thing, too. Tully felt his insides contract. He flicked the ignition and listened to the familiar rumble of the engine. What was Number 19's name? Derek or Drake.

The Mustang squealed out of the parking lot, hell-bent for home. Tully knew he had one last thing to fix before he could fall into bed. He wasn't worried, though. He'd been honing a story for his parents since last night. He'd tell them he'd had too much to drink and had slept in his car. They'd be mad, but they'd believe him.

And after the grand slam in the locker room, this confrontation had to be easy. Had to be.

His sister, Summer, must have heard the Mustang's engine a block away. She was at the back door before Tully turned the knob. He pushed past her and leaned against the wall to take off his shoes.

"You're dead meat, Tulsa," Summer hissed, hovering at his elbow. "Where *were* you all night? Don't think you can slime your way out of this one. Mom and Dad were out of their skulls."

She was crowding him, choking him. Without looking, he put his palm on her forehead and forced her back, not nicely.

"Oh, right, aren't you tough. We'll see how cool you are without the car. They're going to yank it on you, jerk."

Tully was almost numb with exhaustion and anxiety, but he felt a stab under his ribs. Not the car. They wouldn't take away the Mustang. He looked up at Summer and their eyes caught, and he saw for the first time that her face was taut with alarm.

"Tully, where *were* you?" Summer whispered.

"That's what I want to know," Mr. Brown said, stepping into the kitchen.

At first, Tully was relieved that his father had drawn the duty of chewing him out. Of his parents, Tully's mother was the usual disciplinarian. She had the hotter temper, the sharper tongue and the more clearly defined sense of crime and punishment.

His dad was a counselor, in his job and in his life. Tully knew how it would work. He'd get the chance to explain what had happened, and together they'd figure out how to avoid it next time. He might get a lecture, but then he'd get a hug. Tully followed his father into the family room and dropped into his favorite chair, waiting to be counseled.

Make it quick, he pleaded inside himself. He had to sleep and he had to think. But for long moments Mr. Brown only stood, hands in his pockets, looking out the window. Tully noticed that his father's hair was lapping over the back of his collar again. He had to be nagged all the time, to get a decent haircut and trim his beard, and maybe to buy new clothes. Mr. Brown seemed to forget about things like that.

As the silent minutes stretched out, Tully forgot about them, too. Why was this taking so long? Worry pulled him forward in his chair. Please, he thought, not the car. Anything but the car . . .

"I'm so disappointed in you," Mr. Brown said suddenly, softly.

Tully couldn't stop the heat from coming to his cheeks and forehead.

"We gave you a lot of freedom this summer," his father continued, still not looking at him. "God knows, you didn't deserve it, not after last year. But we thought that if we trusted you just once more, treated you like an adult, you'd get your act together."

Tully swallowed, struggling over the knot in his throat. It had been a bad year, a year full of lies and little deceits. A year of bad plunges he hardly remembered, and what he did remember made him wince.

"Damn it," his father said, his knuckles striking the window ledge. "You were doing so good. I was starting to think, 'Yeah, he can handle it. I don't have to watch him every minute.' And then you blew it. Last night."

Something in Tully lurched. "It wasn't my fault, Dad. I—"

His father wheeled to face him, cutting him cold. "Tully, I don't even want to know the story. It doesn't matter if you were stoned or sober or singing in the school choir. You didn't come home and you didn't call." His beard quivered. "I love you, kid, but if you can't live here under our rules, you can't live here. You think about that the next time somebody makes you an offer you can't refuse."

Then he left. And there was no hug. And Tully was left sitting on the edge of his chair with his fingers locked, feeling his pulse throb between his knuckles where his hands met so tightly.

He wished his father had taken away the car.

At two in the afternoon A.J. was shooting baskets in his driveway. It wasn't a challenge. The net over the small garage was at least a foot below regulation height. Without opposition it was just mindless physical activity. A.J. liked mindless activity sometimes. He'd been thinking all morning and he was tired of it.

Thunk, thunk, loft, dunk. Thunk, thunk . . .

A.J. wanted to get as much mileage out of T-shirt weather as possible. This had been the first summer in a long time he'd been able to jump without jiggling.

When you liked your body, A.J. thought, you weren't really aware of it. When you didn't like it, you couldn't think of anything else. Every bulge was like a balloon. You spent your waking life trying to hide it.

Except in hockey. In the bulky pads and oversized jerseys, everyone looked like a gorilla. Nobody cared how he looked anyway; they cared about how he could check. And defensemen were supposed to be a little chunky, right?

But you had to come off the ice sometime. Getting dressed for school had been a horror show. Finding something that fit—and hid what he wanted to hide, and looked halfway decent and wasn't what he had worn the day before—had been more than he could bear some days. A.J. remembered grade ten as two pairs of pants and three sweatshirts. He didn't like to remember it at all. For a lot of reasons, it had been a dark year.

Thunk, thunk, fake, turn. Thunk, loft, dunk.

There was a full-length mirror on the inside of the bathroom door and A.J. found he could look into it now. Not very closely or for very long, but it was a start. When he did look and he saw his skin growing tighter and his shoulders widening and his waist shrinking, he felt a warm ripple run through him. It was the first thing that had worked right in a long time.

He didn't kid himself into thinking he wanted to be a bodybuilder. It was too much work and his heart wasn't in it. His new strength and stamina had accomplished what he wanted. He was on the Cyclones, marginal or not. That was all the body he needed.

One I can put a T-shirt on, A.J. thought. One I can stand to see when I'm coming out of the shower. Just one that somebody could put their arms around and touch, and not laugh.

Last winter, when Tully dated Aimee and Claire and Sandra and Kathy, A.J. went out with Jacquie. She was funny and nice, someone who filled the silent spaces in the conversation and didn't keep saying, "Are you mad at me?"

But she could be quiet, too. In her rec room, when the only light was the glow from the dials on the stereo, Jacquie could be so quiet and acquiescent that there was no mistaking what she didn't say.

It was nice to be hugged and held, but A.J. never asked the question she had already said yes to. I like you, he thought, his face pressed into the warm curve between her shoulder and her ear. I just don't like me enough yet.

Over the summer holidays they stopped dating, and just before fall, Jacquie moved away. A.J. was surprised by how much he missed being held.

"Hi," said a voice behind him. A.J. dropped the ball. He fumbled to retrieve it and turned around.

The man was substantial, but not really big; the green uniform made him look taller than he was. His hair was boyishly thick and so dark it glinted blue under the sun. You couldn't tell his age by his hair, but A.J. could see forty-three years in the creases on the tanned neck, and in the dark smudges under the eyes.

"Hi, Dad," A.J. said.

Decco Brandiosa lifted his hands expectantly, and A.J. bounced the ball to him. They passed it back and forth while A.J. tried to read his father's face, and the eyes that wouldn't meet his. He could sense something, as taut and invisible as a trip wire. He was familiar with this silence. He knew its cold edge. Decco Brandiosa could keep you waiting until you froze.

He ran the last few days over in his head. What had he done, or forgotten to do, that had earned him this? All he could pinpoint was the fact that he had been late last night, very late.

"Well, muscles," Decco said finally. The word curled and twisted out of his mouth. A.J.'s heart leapt.

"Is that what you do it for?" Decco said.

"Do what?" The ball passed between them, once, twice, infuriatingly slow.

"You know," his father said, looking up and pinning him with his eyes. "Whatever it is you do in his basement. The weights."

A.J.'s scalp crawled. He could feel the accusation but he couldn't see it.

"You know my weights are at Tully's," A.J. said, struggling to keep the exasperation from his voice.

"It makes you feel like a big shot? Hey, muscles?" Decco was firing the ball with force now, stinging the boy's bare hands. "It makes you feel like a tough guy?"

"Dad—"

"Shut up." Decco snapped up the ball and held it. "If you had any guts you would have told me first. But, no, I had to hear it on the telephone at work with everybody standing around." His voice was deadly even. "Your own uncle, and you, acting like some kind of street punk. Mike is an old man, A.J. With a heart condi—You look at me!"

A.J.'s head jerked up.

"He's an old man, but I'm not," Decco warned. "You keep throwing your weight around and I'll show you tough, tough guy. Jesus, this makes me sick."

He threw the ball hard, so that it flew past A.J. and onto the lawn. Then he turned and stalked into the house. The boy stared after him, the saliva rising like a bitter flood in his mouth.

The telephone was caught halfway through its first ring.

" 'Lo?" Tully mumbled, trying to prop himself up on his elbow. But the waterbed made it difficult. He sank back on a whoosh of water and cradled the receiver with his shoulder.

"Tul?" A.J. said. Even half asleep Tully recognized the edge in his friend's voice. He tried to sit up again.

"Hi. You okay?"

A.J. heard a faint click and a tinny echo on the line, but he couldn't place it. He started again cautiously. "Tul? I know it's late and everything but can . . . can I come over?"

A voice cut in. "Sorry, A.J. Tully's not supposed to take this call."

Tully sighed. "Summer . . . get off the phone."

"He's grounded," Summer continued blithely on the upstairs extension. "Mom wouldn't let him take a call from the Pope right now."

"Will you—"

"His social life is *finito*. Not that that's a loss or anything, but he's grounded until he's thirty-five. I think they're enrolling him in a monastery on Monday. He'll make a great monk, A.J."

"Yeah, right. You're a real comedienne. How'd you like to do this show with a phone in your mouth?" Tully said, warming up.

"Ooh, I'm scared, macho man," Summer purred. "You know, A.J., he marches around here pretending like he's

Schwarzenegger. You should see this little thing he does in front of the mirror with his neck."

"It's better than what you do in front of the mirror, zit face," Tully said. A.J. could hear his murderous smile. "You know, A.J., I go in there to comb my hair and I have to *wipe* the mirror—"

"You gross pig!" Summer cried.

"I mean, it's just caked on in disgusting little dots. She's a regular zit factory."

"You liar!" Summer said. "If anybody in this house has a zit problem, it's you, jerk! With all that garbage you eat . . ." Her voice trembled.

A.J. sat, glued to a conversation he never had a chance to be involved in. It was like a foreign language, a brother/sister code.

Suddenly there was a shuffling sound, and a new voice broke in.

"Okay, Tully, put a lid on it," Mrs. Brown said with a short, sharp sigh. "You know, I'm really not happy with you right now, and I get so tired of you tormenting her—"

"Tormenting her!" Tully bristled. "You tell that suckhole not to dish it out if she can't take it. And besides, this was my phone call. She cut into *my* call."

There was a brief silence, then . . . "Hello, who's on the line?" Mrs. Brown asked, her voice rising an octave.

A.J. jumped. He felt like a voyeur. "Uh, it's A.J., Mrs. Brown."

"Tully will call you tomorrow," Mrs. Brown said, polite but firm. *"If* he grows up a little."

"Hey," Tully blurted. "This is important. You can't just

cut off my call. Give me one minute to finish up. One minute!"

There was a moment's hesitation. "Thirty seconds, Tully," Mrs. Brown said evenly, "and then I'm picking up the phone and you had better not be on it."

"Yeah, yeah," the boy muttered.

"Thirty seconds," she warned again, and then she hung up, and the line was quiet and clear. A.J. wound the telephone cord around one of his fingers, waiting.

"Life stinks," Tully said. Then his voice softened. "Look, come over tomorrow, as soon as you can get away. We'll do some lifting or something."

"But what about—"

"Don't worry, they'll let you in. They like you," Tully said. "Probably more than they like me right now."

And at that moment, A.J. did feel liked. Crouched in the darkened hallway with the phone warm against his ear, he felt liked for the first time all day.

"Okay," he said. "I'll be there."

When he'd hung up, he sat for a moment, leaning against the wall. His father was ironing shirts in the living room. A.J. could hear the creak, creak of the ironing board and the sharp hiss of steam.

Why were some houses so easy to be in, he wondered. How many evenings had he stayed late at Tully's, too comfortable to get up and leave? He liked the sound of them, the way they fit together, even when they fought.

A.J. knew that whatever had been bugging Tully after hockey practice, he could handle it. Living in a real family taught you how to fight back. The other kind of family, A.J. thought, just taught you how to duck.

· FOUR ·

THERE WAS A ritual to getting dressed for a game. For some guys it started outside the rink. Mendel always tapped the door three times before he entered. Millyard put his skates on first, before anything, even his jock strap. To an outsider it would have looked ridiculous, a naked young man in skates, but nobody on the team even looked twice. Everybody had their quirks.

For A.J., it was the way he taped his stick. He did it last, after he was dressed. He'd find an empty corner and sit down with his fabric tape—black for the bottom, white for the top—and start winding, silent, intent. If somebody spoke to him, the words bounced off. Once the process had started, he was in a trance until it was complete.

He always began with the black tape on the blade of the stick, five or six rows to hide the puck. Some guys, the hotshots, did only two rows, but ever since he could remember, A.J. had liked the solid section of black across the blade.

The taping of the top half was more crucial. It could take him twenty minutes and a whole roll of white tape to get it right. He began with the knob, the careful ball of tape at the top of the handle that would help him hang on to the stick. He'd anchor the tape to the stick, then pull out an arm's length from the roll, spinning it into twine for the bulk the knob needed. He'd spin another arm's length and repeat the process until the size and shape were right. Then he'd begin wrapping the tape smooth over the knob and hand grip.

A.J. never remembered what he thought about while he taped his stick; he tried not to think at all. But that Saturday night of their first game against the North Battleford Kings, he couldn't keep his head clear. When he tried to get rid of the doubts, they bounced back at him.

He had only two fears: that he wouldn't get on the ice, and that he would, and screw up.

It's just exhibition, for Pete's sake, A.J. told himself. But he knew it wasn't. Moose Jaw cared about Triple A.

The whole province was passionate about it. Saskatchewan didn't have an NHL hockey team. What it had were winters so long and bleak they bordered on madness. It had kids who started pushing kitchen chairs around the ice at the age of four, and parents who could break into fistfights in the stands. Minor hockey was something to devour in the hungriest, emptiest months of the year. A.J. knew that if he got on the ice at all, people would be watching him.

And so would Landau. A.J. had had one, maybe two good plays in practice, but the rest of the week had been mediocre. Marginal.

The taping finished, A.J. ripped off the roll with one deft movement, and dropped it on the bench beside him.

Tape was expensive, but he never used the same roll of white twice. It was another quirk.

Clang! Startled, A.J. dropped his stick.

"Hook shot!" Tully cried, and fired another empty tape roll into the metal garbage can. *Clang!* "The crowd goes wild."

A.J. grinned and retrieved his stick. "Dr. J, I presume."

Tully snatched an empty drink can from the bench and faked a pass. "The sultan of smooth," he said, tossing the can in a gentle arch. *Ting!* It hit the rim and skidded over the spongy black floor.

"Don't give up your day job," A.J. said.

Tully's feet were bare. He never put on socks and skates until the last minute. He was so hyperactive before a game that it was maddening for him to clunk around in skates.

Now he lifted a foot onto the bench beside A.J. and leaned forward, resting on his knee. "You coming out with us after?"

"Who's us?"

"You know, Weitzammer, Mendel, some girls—just a bunch of us. It's no big deal. Maybe we'll just go get a pizza or something."

"Who are you going with?"

"Andrea Knutson," Tully said, but he was interrupted by a loud groan. A young man who was almost un-recognizable under his equipment gave Tully a solid whack on the leg with his stick.

"Knutson? You're killing me, Brown. I have been trying to get to that girl for weeks."

"So I'm charming, what can I say?" Tully tossed his head.

"It's the car," the young man sighed. "It's gotta be the

car." He thunked Tully with his stick again and drifted away. The blond boy turned back to his friend, and his voice dropped just a shade.

"Summer's coming, too," Tully said.

"So?" A.J. said. The word came out too fast.

Tully's mouth twisted into a knowing smile. He shrugged.

"Summer," A.J. said. He tried to make it sound like a question, but he couldn't. "Get real."

"Hey, I'm insulted. She drives me nuts sometimes, but she is my sister. Family pride."

A.J. had picked up the roll of white tape and was fiddling with it, curling back the sticky edge. Was he so obvious that the whole world could see it, even when he tried to be careful? Or did Tully just read him because he was Tully?

"Don't fix me up, Tul."

"So who's fixing?" Tully was defensive. "I'm making a statement. You said, 'Who's going?' and I told you. That's not fixing."

For a moment the only sound was the muted buzz of the locker room. They heard Grummett tell someone to be sure to swing out wide for the pass.

"You're crazy," A.J. said at last. "She hates me."

"Aw, no, she doesn't. She's like that with everybody."

A.J. looked up, but he couldn't keep the faint smirk off his face. "Liar."

Luckily, Landau came in then and started prepping them. A.J. was grateful for the diversion. He sat with the rest of the team while Landau went over the North Battleford lines, cautioning them about one of the defensemen, and a center.

"Don't underestimate him," Landau pushed. "The guy looks like a badminton racquet but he's as slippery as a greased worm. Don't turn your back on him. He wants to play footsie? Give him the message."

A.J. listened and watched. He was good at focusing. When it came time to play, usually he could put everything else out of his mind. Except now he kept shifting on the bench, trying to shrug off the uncomfortable warmth that flushed through him like a memory.

He'd known Summer as long as he'd known Tully, but he'd never completely relaxed around her. Summer said what she was thinking, and you never knew what she'd think next.

A.J. had no sisters. Even before his mother left, he had never run into wet stockings hanging in the bathroom; he'd never knocked over cosmetics on the vanity. Everything Alina Brandiosa had was tucked so neatly away, like her high heels at the very back of the hall closet, it was as if she'd been half packed for years.

And so A.J. watched Summer. Not straight out, and not when she was looking—he was so careful. But he absorbed her. The way she moved, the way she sounded. And he wasn't exactly sure when it had stopped being watching and started being something else.

Once, last year, when the Browns were renovating the main floor, A.J. had gone upstairs to use the second-floor bathroom. The door to Summer's room was open, and there was no one home except Tully in the basement. The sunlight from her window spilled onto the hall carpet by his feet.

He'd just wanted to see. Where her things were, and where she slept. A.J. had stood in the doorway and looked at the rumpled quilt and the drinking glasses all over the dresser. There was a poster of David Bowie that reminded him faintly of Tully, and there were clothes abandoned recklessly on the bed and chair and floor. A yellow T-shirt caught his eye.

He'd only come in for a quick glance, but all of a sudden the T-shirt was in his hand. It was soft cotton, not flimsy like his own, but heavier and softer. Before he could even think, the T-shirt was against his face and he was breathing in the scent of Summer.

She smelled of sweat, salty but not sharp, and of outside. Grass. She smelled like the last day in August when you played football on the lawn. The heat grew inside him so gently, so cautiously, that he didn't even notice until it hurt.

There was a faint noise, a distant scraping from downstairs, but it jarred him. To be caught in here, feeling like this . . .

A.J. threw the shirt down and bolted into the bathroom. It was some minutes before he could face his friend without embarrassing himself. But even when he was back to normal and could start down the stairs, the sensation rippled in him like an echo.

You could date a friend's sister, A.J. thought. You could date her and you could like her. But to date her and feel like this, that was dangerous.

North Battleford was dangerous, too. It didn't matter that it was only exhibition. They tore into the game hungry for ice. The forwards were fast and sly, and caught the Cyclones' front line by surprise. The Moose Jaw goalie, Terry

Frances, jumped and dove far more than he should have in the first ten minutes of play.

"Jesus Christ," he spat at his defense, "if you're just here to watch, go sit in the stands. You're blocking my view."

Halfway through the first period, though, the Cyclones began to click. It was little things—completed passes and sharp interceptions. They managed to move the puck better, and they moved it more often into the North Battleford zone.

Landau hadn't played A.J. at all, but he sent him in at the end of the first period. The boy had been suffering on the bench and now he checked and blocked with intensity, forcing the North Battleford forwards wide when they learned to duck him.

He had one good play. It was the final minutes of a scoreless first period. The Cyclones had been worrying the puck in the Kings' zone, unable to get a clear shot. Tully, against the boards at the blue line, finally maneuvered around the winger who'd been covering him. He passed to Weitzammer, but the puck was intercepted by the North Battleford center. The winger who'd been shadowing Tully dropped back to receive the pass, then whirled around to the open ice.

Stationed at the North Battleford blue line, A.J. saw the play before it happened. He'd been watching the center, not the puck, and the second he saw him flinch to scoop it, A.J. started backing up.

He needed the head start. The winger was fast, and as soon as he had the puck on his stick he was away, hurtling towards the Moose Jaw net. Breakaway.

The home crowd was up, screaming, but A.J. couldn't hear it. He dug into the ice, scrambling to catch the gold and blue jersey that was only a blur in his eyes. He knew there wouldn't be time to force the winger wide. He had to take either the puck or the player.

He caught him just beyond the Moose Jaw blue line. A.J. saw the twitch, the windup for the slapshot, and lunged. The puck stayed where it was and the winger flew.

No one had to tell him it was a great play, but they did. A.J. sailed into the dressing room on the sound of thunder, buffeted by the solid pounding of leather gloves. Even Landau cuffed him.

"Nice piece of work, Brandiosa."

But the momentum didn't hold. North Battle came into the second period cheated and hungry. They picked up the pace and put on the pressure, digging in with shoulders and elbows and the occasional stick.

It was in the second period that A.J. met the Worm.

His number was 5, and he was small, even for a center. With his bandy legs and flapping jersey, he was laughable. But he was everything else Landau had said, too.

When the puck was in the Moose Jaw end and A.J. was scuffling against the boards, the Worm stayed well back. But the moment the puck was flying down the ice and everyone was watching the North Battleford net, Number 5 tripped him. Hard.

A.J. tumbled, his stick skidding, and came up cursing. But the Worm was long gone. And of course the referee was watching the play. A.J. let it go, but the next time the two were on the ice together, Number 5 hooked him again. And again.

A.J. came off his shift spitting blue. Landau watched him bluster and sputter for a few minutes, and he couldn't hold back the I-told-you-so gleam from his eyes.

"You've got a problem, Brandiosa?" Landau said finally. The corners of his mouth quivered.

"Yeah, I got a problem—a *bug* problem," A.J. seethed. "There's this freakin' insect with a big number five on its back!"

"That skinny little guy is giving you trouble? What do you weigh, kid—180?"

A.J. could hear the chuckle in Landau's voice. "Hey, come on. The guy is a . . . a . . ."

"Worm?" Landau supplied, his mouth twisting. Then his features hardened again. "If you've got a problem, solve it. But we can afford five minutes, not two." And he turned away.

A.J. sat on the bench, melting the ice with his eyes. Landau had made himself clear. A fighting penalty was five minutes, but the player was replaced on the ice. A two-minute penalty for roughing would leave his team short-handed. A.J. didn't want two minutes and he didn't want five. He just wanted to give the Worm some of his own medicine.

A.J. and the center weren't on the ice together until halfway through the third period. The setup had to be perfect, A.J. knew. If it wasn't done exactly right, he'd get two minutes for sure.

He was watching the North Battleford center so intently, he missed seeing the only goal of the night.

It wasn't beautiful but nobody cared. It was a mishmash of a goal, all elbows and sticks and cursing in the North Battleford zone. Mendel to Tully to Mendel to Rudachuk —who should have shot but didn't have the nerve—back to Tully, who finally squeezed it in.

The crowd, almost as sweaty and wrung out as the players, cheered with exultation and relief. And even though he had no part in the goal, didn't even *see* it, A.J. was lifted by the inevitable rush. They were ahead, and the game was almost over. He was soaked with power.

"Come on, Worm," he coaxed under his breath. And at last the Worm came.

North Battleford was panicking and put the pressure on in a rush of their own. The puck skittered back and forth between the Moose Jaw blue line and center ice. Number Five, looking for an easy trick, moved over and stationed himself to the left of the Cyclones' net. A.J. was on him like a shadow, trying to shove him out of position and keep the goalie's view clear. The Worm dug in and held his ground.

As soon as the puck and the players were heading back towards the North Battleford end, Number Five moved to follow. But A.J. had hooked his leg solidly behind the center's left one and the Worm flipped backwards onto the ice. A.J. slammed down on top of him, all 176 pounds. Elbows first. And while Number Five turned white and gasped for breath, A.J. pushed himself up on the center's stomach, hard.

"You trip me again and you'll be chewing this goddamn stick," he hissed into the boy's face. And the Worm got the message, at last.

There were no more goals, and the Cyclones staggered into the dressing room on the giddy, strung-out high of winners. A.J. scrubbed the sweat off himself in the shower. He felt like singing. He had hammered out a little space for himself in this place with these people, and he knew it was going to be his best year ever.

Outside the arena, though, he didn't feel quite the same. Andrea held the Mustang's bucket seat so that A.J. could crawl in behind. He hesitated—the back seat wasn't his regular place—then slid in. It seemed dark in there, dark and close. He stared straight at the back of Andrea's head, but every now and then the passing streetlights would catch on Summer's knees or the metal clips of her jacket, and once, her hair. He saw her in fragments out of the corner of his eye, and couldn't help but assemble them in his mind.

She ignored him, or almost. After a hearty "Hi, A.J.!" —to let him and the whole car know that he was only her brother's friend and she saw him as often as Mondays— Summer let him fall off the edge of a cliff. All the way to the pizza place she talked to Andrea and teased Tully about his driving.

"Just for a change, try the brake. You remember—it's the *other* pedal?

"Now, you may want to call the minister of highways on this one, Tulsa, but isn't it considered bad manners to drive into the oncoming lane?"

She had Andrea giggling and Tully rolling his eyes. A.J. sat, his hands burrowed into his jacket pockets. I'm in the wrong seat, he thought. I'm in the wrong car. I'm in the wrong life. He felt big and clumsy, overgrown.

They had just moved into the doorway of the restaurant when Al Weitzammer stood up at a table and waved them over. From across the room, A.J. could see the table was already full. There were guys from school as well as the team, and girls. They'd have to push another table over.

Smooth as anything, Tully took Andrea's hand and threaded his way through the crowded restaurant. A.J. expected Summer to jump in ahead of him, close behind her brother. But she didn't. She clasped the back of A.J.'s jacket, balled up a small piece in her fist, and pushed him in front of her. He was so surprised to feel her hand on him that he almost walked into a chair.

They talked hockey from the moment they sat down. The game was replayed in fast forward and slow motion. Everyone made a fuss over Tully, which was to be expected. What startled A.J. was that they made a fuss over him, too. His checks and passes and, of course, his great play in the first period.

Harold Doerkson from school, all knuckles and elbows and lecherous grin, kept leaning across the table.

"Once you were over center ice, you had him," Doerkson said. "The sucker didn't have a prayer. Bammo! Hot streak, Brandiosa."

Somebody elbowed Doerkson and glanced at Summer. Together they looked back at A.J., their eyes telling him he was still on a hot streak.

A.J. had forgotten all about her. He'd been so busy absorbing the unusual attention, he hadn't noticed that Summer hadn't said a word since they'd sat down.

A.J. turned cautiously, the first time he'd looked at her with both eyes all evening. She was still wearing her jacket, an oversized royal purple thing. It seemed to swallow her. She kept her arms tucked in at her sides and toyed with a napkin in her lap, rolling and unrolling one of the corners. Only her chin stuck out defiantly.

A.J. touched her arm, clearly a question.

Summer eyed him guardedly. "I despise hockey," she said.

"Yeah, me, too," A.J. said.

There was silence, then a clear, surprised laugh that almost lifted him out of his shoes.

"Well, it's a good thing you weren't playing it or anything."

"Right," A.J. said. "That was professional wrestling."

Summer laughed again.

"Just call me Crusher," he said.

A.J. wasn't naturally funny like Tully, but tonight he felt buoyant enough for anything.

"So what do you think of the commodities market?" Summer asked, her eyes twinkling wickedly.

"Just great," A.J. said, playing along. " 'Specially now that people got them *indoor* commodities. They're selling them commodities like hot cakes."

He knew he was surprising her. He surprised himself. Her laughter lit him up so much he had to look away to keep his face straight.

He glanced across the table. Tully was riding high. Strangers craned their necks, wondering who was celebrating. But Andrea was clearly his biggest fan, watching him with shy, admiring eyes. That dog, A.J. grinned. He never misses.

Tully felt strong. To be with the guys, a girl on his arm and a goal under his belt, made him feel safe.

There would be no more trouble with Number 19. Early that week he had taken steps to make sure of it. He had gambled, and won.

On Tuesday Tully had skipped his last class and driven to St. Augustus, a separate school. He'd parked across the street from the main doors, turned off the engine, and waited. At first he was icy cool, determined, but as the minutes dragged on he jumped at every sound, every passing car. The skin on the back of his neck tingled.

When the bell finally sounded, he scrunched down. He did not want to see anyone he knew. He kept a careful eye on the crowd of kids that poured out through the doors and onto the sidewalk.

Derek Lavalle came out with the last group of stragglers; that was his style. Tully knew he didn't have to move. The red Mustang was like a flag. Smirking, Derek adjusted the collar of his jacket and slowly, slowly sauntered over. He stood on the pavement, as if he were admiring the car.

Tully couldn't bring himself to look into the gray eyes, and he knew that was a mistake. But he still had a few cards to play. Without warning, he leaned across the passenger seat and unlocked the door, then he pushed it open with his foot. It hung ajar for ten achingly long seconds. Finally, Derek moved. He walked deliberately around the car and swung into the passenger seat. Tully felt a small gush of relief, even triumph. He had guessed right.

He didn't let down his guard, though. Close in the car, he could still sense danger, its scent as keen as sulfur. But this kind of danger was different. It was unpredictable, exciting. His nerves were awake and he could feel his own power humming through his body. Wordlessly he flicked the ignition, and the Mustang surged into life.

Now, four days later, Tully was enjoying a hangover of leftover sensation, buoyed by the energy of the night. The game had been great, the goal had been great. He and Derek had come to terms. Easy terms. Tully squeezed Andrea closer to him and impulsively kissed her on the side of the head, just above her ear. She looked at him quizzically, but he didn't care. He kissed her again and this time she laughed, and so did everyone else. It was giddy, light-hearted. Almost like being in love.

• FIVE •

IT WAS A Thursday night in early October, and it was cold. Never mind the calendar. In A.J.'s heart it was already winter, and every time he looked up at the solid sheet of gray sky, he expected snow.

They'd been "setting the house right," he and his father. Decco never called it housecleaning, and before Alina had left, he'd never done it. Now A.J. was surprised by how easily his father could whisk through a stack of dirty dishes, or buff up a shine on the cabinets. He'd known all along, the faker, A.J. thought.

"Here, before you go, grab the other end of this," Decco said. Already in his jacket, A.J. dropped his leather biking gloves and reached down for a solid grip on the Hide-A-Bed that doubled as a couch. It was ancient, and unbelievably heavy. There were no rolling casters; you couldn't push it. The very few times a year it was moved, to vacuum the rug underneath, were pure penance.

Both men took a breath. "All right, at the count of

three . . ." Decco said. A.J. heaved and felt the muscles in his stomach and pelvis tighten angrily. The two inched crablike towards the door.

"Over there," Decco grimaced, his dark hair dangling over his forehead. A.J. knew he was strong, but by the time the hide-a-bed was over by the wall, his shoulder sockets were screaming, and he could feel the great rhinoceros sliding out of his grasp. It came down with a bang, the sound echoing through the metalwork inside.

They both leaned on the arms, gasping. "Jeez . . . I . . . hate this thing," A.J. muttered. Decco nodded.

"What are you vacuuming for, anyway?" the boy asked when his breath came back. "Trying to sell the house?"

"No," his father said, straightening up slowly. But there was the oddest look about him, an unfamiliar look. Almost shy.

A.J. was intrigued. "Dad . . . ?"

"It's just time, that's all. Where are you going, anyway?"

A.J. picked up his black and yellow gloves again. "Tully's. We're going to push some weight."

"All right. Don't be late." He tugged on the boy's jacket collar. "No beer, hey?"

A.J. rolled his eyes, but the warning was good-natured, affectionate. The door banged lightly behind him as he left.

It wasn't late—just before eight o'clock—but the sky was dark. The pavement was coated with a damp mist that glistened under the streetlamps. It was like being in a movie.

A.J. whipped his bike effortlessly around the corners. He would rather have had a car—who wouldn't?—but it was a good bike. A Raleigh. He didn't even mind the cold air that bit his ears and stung his nose.

His father had been in an exceptional mood this last while. A.J. had been cautious; he knew Decco's roller-coaster moods too well—the slow, jerking ascent and the gut-wrenching plunge. But as the days passed and the plunge didn't come, A.J. carefully, carefully relaxed.

The night was singing in him as he glided through the streets. He was looking forward to the evening. He hadn't seen much of Tully lately, and he was hungry for a workout, and talk. Maybe Summer would drift down the stairs and shoot the breeze with them. He'd like that. He'd like it a lot. After their almost-date a few weeks ago, she'd been a little warmer. Not really nice, but warmer. For now, that was enough.

A tiny piece of his mind was uneasy. He hadn't called Tully's house to make sure his friend was there. Tully had been disappearing lately, taking off without telling anyone.

Summer answered the door.

"He's out, A.J.," she said.

"Again?" A.J. felt something inside him sink.

"Again." Summer moved, not quite a shrug, but a gesture of confusion.

"He's okay," A.J. said, pretending to study the door hinge.

"Yeah, sure," Summer said softly. "It's just . . . you know."

And he did know. They had so much history behind them, A.J., Summer and Tully. Sometimes A.J. wished they didn't. Sometimes, like now, he wished he and Summer were just starting, with no history at all.

"Is he with Andrea?" A.J. asked.

Summer shook her head. "I don't think so. She called here earlier and left a message for him."

He could feel her eyes on him, expecting.

"What do you want me to do?"

"Just go look," Summer said. "You know him. Just look around. And check."

She didn't say what he was to check for. That was part of history, too. His insides felt clogged, like a stream choked with silt. But her worry was an echo of his own now.

"Okay." The leather of his jacket creaked as he moved. "I'll look."

She caught his arm. "And you'll tell me, right?"

"Right," he said. "I'll tell you."

He started a slow sweep of the likely neighborhoods, gliding down back lanes. An outsider would think you could hide one person in a city of 40,000, but A.J. knew better. It was the same as a town of 4,000, or 400. You couldn't really hide anything. There were eight old Mustangs in Moose Jaw. Three were notchback '69's. Only one was red.

He felt rotten spying on Tully. He wasn't Tully's mother. They were just friends. Best friends. But you didn't let a friend make the same mistake twice.

Last year Tully had a problem. It was a coming-home problem, it was a getting-to-school problem. Sometimes it was a walking problem. It was definitely a staying-awake problem.

Someone else might have pulled it off, but the difference was too big for A.J. not to notice. Tully was usually so hyperactive, so alive, that to see him drifting through his days set off the warning signals in A.J.'s head.

It made him angry because it was weak. And A.J. had seen weak. He'd seen it most clearly in the faces of what he called Space Cadets.

Space Cadets were the swaybacked young thugs who worked at the trainyards, when they worked at all. Most were in their twenties, unshaven and stringy, with brains like pomegranates. Space Cadets showed up at parties everywhere, proud of their full-throttle lives. But they were from another planet, another sphere.

Or so he had thought.

One day, while he'd been waiting in the car for Tully, A.J. had seen a flash of silver stuck between the seats. Curious, he'd reached down and dug out a butter knife.

It was new and shiny, except for the top two inches of the blade that were black. A.J. knew that if he combed through the car, he would find the knife's twin, and probably a large wine bottle with the bottom broken out.

This kind of knife led only one life, slated through the rings of a stove element. When they were glowing red they were clasped together to crush little chunks of hash that disintegrated into pungent clouds of smoke. The wine bottle was used as a convenient inhaler. A.J. had seen the whole performance a dozen times, and he had never gotten over how stupid people looked, hunched over a stove element. It made him sick.

He curled his fingers around the handle of the discolored knife. He heard Tully get in and pull the door shut with a solid bang.

"Okay, let's go," Tully said, firing up the engine. A.J. didn't reply; he just held the knife. Tully glanced over and took a breath, but nothing was said as the Mustang surged out into the flow of traffic.

"Planning for a new career, Tul?" A.J. said finally. "Opening a restaurant maybe? Looks like you've already got the utensils. For something."

Tully laughed nervously. "It's those damn hoodlums, officer. Always hanging around the back lane. My wife found it in the yard."

But A.J. wasn't playing. "Get real, Tulsa. Every time I see you, you're stoned. You're like a bloody zombie. I hardly know you anymore. What a great life, Tul."

Tully's face hardened and he leaned heavy on the gas. "Why, thank you, Mr. Clean. You've changed my life. How did I ever live sixteen years without you?"

"I can't believe you're this stupid, Tul," A.J. said. "I really thought you had more on the ball than a Space Cadet. Why don't you just save yourself time and drop out of school and start collecting unemployment now? Beat the rush?"

"That's right, keep talking. You're real good at that, A.J. It's listening you have a problem with." Tully's voice was taut with bitterness. "You're so goddamned self-centered you don't even know I'm here half the time. I feel like your *chauffeur*. Call me a Space Cadet, but maybe I'm just lonely."

It was like a check from his blind side that sent A.J. sailing into the boards. It crushed him into silence.

He had forgotten that Tully was good at this. Growing up in a real family, fencing was second nature to him. A.J. plowed straight ahead in an argument; Tully looked for a pressure point. This time he had hit it, dead on. It was a long while before A.J. could speak.

But he didn't give up, and he wasn't alone. Tully's parents had grown up in the drug-drenched sixties, and they had first-hand ammunition. They also knew about some pressure points themselves. Mr. and Mrs. Brown rode Tully continually—nothing vicious, but constant. And they did it in front of A.J., and anyone else who happened to be there. Summer was allowed to go to every party with Tully, as his chaperone, and she threw herself into the role with vigor. A.J. gave up his frontal attack and settled on needling.

They outnumbered him, and wore Tully down. Or maybe he simply grew bored with it, or maybe he got tired of taking Summer on every date. Or maybe something else happened. Whatever it was, it finally worked.

Or did it, A.J. wondered, wheeling his bike towards downtown. It had been five or six months that Tully had been his regular self, but did you ever really know somebody? What if he did spot the red Mustang, what would he say? Hi, Tul, just making sure you're on the straight and narrow? You weren't supposed to spy on friends.

He spent twenty minutes cruising the downtown area, sailing past fast-food joints and the empty parking lots where kids and cars usually clustered. He didn't see any old Mustangs, let alone Tully's red '69, and he was starting to feel stupid, and cold. The tips of his fingers were numb, and his head hummed with a dull ache.

He was just turning around to start home, when he saw it, the snub back end of a red Mustang, parked in a side street. A.J. swung his bike around in the middle of the empty road and pulled up beside the car, his heart hammering. It was empty, but it was Tully's; A.J. recognized the squashed Burger King bag on the floor in the back.

A.J. looked left and right and finally chained his bike to a No Parking sign. This was the very edge of downtown and unfamiliar to him. On one side of the street there were a few dark buildings—dusty, semi-industrial places. A spring service place, a shoe repair, a grimy establishment called The Oh Boy Lunch. It was closed. The other side of the street was an empty field, stretching eerily back towards the train yards. A.J. peered down the sidewalk and made out a patch of light from a window, half a block away. When he got there, he discovered it was a pool hall and coffee bar called Chicco's.

I'll just go in and warm up, A.J. thought. If he's there, okay. If not, I'll forget the whole thing and go home.

When he pushed open the door, the warmth and light made his eyes gloss over, the way people's eyeglasses fogged. He took off his biking gloves and flexed his fingers, standing in the doorway. But he didn't want it to seem like he was looking for somebody, so he walked to the coffee bar and settled onto one of the swivel seats. Behind him he could hear the sharp *crack, crack* of pool balls, and the sound of young men kidding each other. The waitress wandered over.

"Hot chocolate," A.J. said. "No . . . uh, coffee." He'd been trying to drink more coffee lately. It seemed older.

As soon as the waitress was gone, he twisted sideways and turned his attention to the pool table area. He was very casual. If he did find Tully, he wanted it to look like an accident.

A.J. glanced around, trying not to stare. It looked like most pool rooms—dim, perhaps cleaner than most. There were six of the big green tables and racks of cues. There were cheap wooden chairs, tin ashtrays and, of course, guys playing pool. Most of them were young, maybe his age, maybe older. And there were a few punkers. A.J. instantly recognized the high spiked hair and black clothes, like a uniform. He relaxed.

It seemed okay, not a biker hangout or a hotbed of organized crime. If Tully came down to this neighborhood to shoot a little pool by himself or whatever, so what?

He heard his coffee being set on the counter behind him and turned back to it. Taking a sip, he looked at the other end of the counter and noticed for the first time he wasn't alone. There were two guys sitting together. They were so close that their shoulders touched, in the familiar way of people who knew each other, very well.

They're queer, A.J. thought suddenly. As the information registered in his brain, a pulse of electricity ran through his body, bursting painfully in his fingertips. Slowly, he eased his chair around and looked back at the pool room.

The room was the same, but his vision had changed. It seemed to him that the atmosphere was different from other pool rooms he'd been in. There wasn't the standoffishness, the usual coolness of a group of men. The pool players seemed to kid each other more, touch each other more. And against the far wall in a darkened corner, he could make out two figures, pressed tightly together.

A.J. whirled back to his coffee, his fists clenched. I'm in a freaking queer joint—me!—in a queer joint! Anybody comes over, I'll deck him, A.J. thought savagely, even though no one had moved towards him or really looked his way. He stood up abruptly and pulled a crumpled bill out of his front jeans pocket. His eyes were so glazed he didn't know if it was a one or a five. He tossed the money onto the counter beside the almost-full cup of coffee, and headed for the door.

In three strides he was at the entranceway, and pushed
his way out onto the sidewalk. He almost slammed into
Tully, who'd been reaching for the door. Number 19 was
with him, his arm resting across Tully's shoulders, his hand
draped casually against Tully's neck.

A.J. stood for a moment, staring stupidly. His eyes
seemed to focus on Tully's neck, on the hand that touched
the bare skin so carelessly. There were no words connected
to the picture he saw. He felt as distant as a dream.

The color had drained from Tully's face, and his eyes
flashed suddenly emerald under the false light of the streetlamps.

"A.J.," he whispered. A.J. felt the word like a knee. A
curdling sensation spread outwards from his gut. He turned
and lurched down the street, not looking behind him, not
even once. At his bike, he struggled with the lock. There
seemed to be no sensation in his fingers.

"Come on, come on!" he muttered to himself. Terror
was rising in the back of his throat, terror that he would
hear footsteps on the pavement behind him. The moment
the bike was free, he was up on it, wheeling down the
street. But he couldn't seem to get his balance. He swayed
and swerved as if he were drunk.

The wind screamed past his ears and tore at his chest.
He'd left his jacket open and had forgotten the biking
gloves on the counter of the coffee bar. He was vaguely
aware that he was freezing, but he didn't care. His arms
were like pieces of wood that attached him to the bike, and
his legs pedaled numbly, desperately.

Suddenly a car horn blasted beside him, and he veered
sharply. The bike jackknifed and he tumbled, his hands
skidding over the asphalt.

The car's brakes screeched and a man leapt out. "Oh, my God, oh, my God! Are you all right?"

A.J. sat up blankly.

"You were all over the road," the man moaned, reaching to help the boy up. "What's the matter with you? Are you on drugs or something, kid?"

Now the pain registered, gouging him. He wrenched himself out of the man's grasp.

"Screw you," he spat, holding his hands away from him as if they were clubs. The man stepped back, frightened.

"It was an accident, kid. You were all over the road, for cryin' out loud. Maybe we should get you to the hospital."

"Screw you!" A.J. screamed, and the water that sprang to his eyes burned him, blinded him. The man scrambled back into his car, but stuck his head out of the window as he revved the engine.

"You're sick, kid. You should get to the hospital!" A.J. leapt at the car and kicked the door with the heel of his boot. Hard. He felt the metal dent. The car roared away, tires squealing.

For a minute A.J. just stood by the side of the road, shaking. He wiped his eyes on the sleeve of his jacket, fighting the urge to break down and sob. His hands were on fire.

"Get home," he muttered to himself. "Just get home." He brushed the loose stones from his hands and managed to get up on his bike. He leaned forward on the handlebars, resting on the edge of his palms. A picture burned in the very back of his brain, but he wouldn't look at it.

· SIX ·

TULLY STOOD IN the doorway of Chicco's like a manne-
quin. His power of movement had been yanked away on
the sidewalk, when the first thunderbolt of shock had
driven up from his stomach to his throat.

I knew this was coming, he thought, watching the back
of A.J.'s jacket until it disappeared. God damn it, I *knew*.
But knowing never made you ready. There were some
things you couldn't rehearse.

Derek finally steered him through the doors and over to
the coffee counter, just a few seats from A.J.'s full cup.
Tully saw the black and yellow biking gloves and picked
them up, imagining what had happened. He could almost
feel the aftershock still rolling outwards from the chair.

Tully ordered a Coke and sat, watching the bubbles rise
to the surface. Derek ordered a chocolate float and drank
the whole thing, noisily, with a straw. After a few minutes, he took hold of the back of Tully's jean jacket and
tugged, just once.

"I think the big bad defense just had his perspective widened," Derek said. "Think he'll recover?"

His voice was icy with practiced disregard. Tully, who was usually intrigued by that mean streak, wasn't. Right now he hated it.

"Could you take a crash course in being human?" Tully said, staring at the counter. "That was my friend."

"Oh, right. Your *friend.*" Derek put an ugly slant on the word. Tully fought the urge to hit him.

A.J. had been a raw spot between them from the start. Derek was sarcastic about how much time A.J. spent in the Mustang, and the weight set in Tully's basement.

"How cozy," he'd smirked.

Tully had tried to explain, and gave up. Derek had lovers and acquaintances and enemies. He certainly had no one like A.J.

Now maybe I don't, either, Tully thought. He felt sick.

Derek sighed irritably. "I don't understand what you're so worried about," he said. "Did you see his face? The kid's not *capable* of telling anyone. And if he could, who would he tell? The Yearbook Committee? *Junior Hockey News?*"

I'm worried about what he thinks, not what he says, Tully thought. But it was useless to tell Derek. The blond boy stood up abruptly.

"I have to go," he said.

Derek swiveled around, alarmed, but he caught himself and shrugged. "I'll call you," he said.

"No," Tully blurted out, his voice rising so sharply that a few people looked over. He hesitated, wringing the soft leather biking gloves. "I'll call you."

"When?"

When it's better, Tully thought. When I don't feel so

bad I want to puke. When I've talked to him and smoothed it out and got it to where he understands, a little.

"When I'm good and ready," Tully said.

Derek shrugged and reached for Tully's untouched glass of Coke. He slid it smoothly across the counter and began to drink it. But when Tully had turned, Derek set down the glass and watched him go, his gray eyes as alert as a lynx's.

Tully drove around until almost midnight. He turned up the heat in the Mustang, but he kept having chills— tremors that made his scalp crawl as they ran over him. It felt like the flu.

He found himself driving the streets dangerously close to A.J.'s house. He knew he had a legitimate excuse—the biking gloves that lay on the passenger seat—but it was late. He was ashamed of his desire to fix it *now*.

A.J. frustrated the hell out of him sometimes. He was stubborn and single-minded and self-absorbed. He was also one of the sanest people Tully knew. A.J. never played mind games. Tully knew he could just be with A.J. and not worry about what he was saying, or how he was acting. It was such a relief. These last couple of years, with his dad and everything, A.J. had leaned on him. But Tully knew he had been leaning, too.

When the boy finally pulled into his own driveway, the house was dark and silent. He went straight into the family room and fumbled through his cartoon videocassettes. Tully loved cartoons, and he was hungry for something that would make him stop thinking. He plunked in a whole tape of Huckleberry Hound and slumped onto the couch. He didn't turn on the lights; he didn't take off his jacket.

Summer came in in her housecoat. "You're late," she said. "You're going to get grounded. Mom and Dad say go to bed."

"No," he said, the strain pulling the word apart. He winced.

Summer paused and took a step closer. "Tully . . . is something wrong?"

He shook his head roughly.

She took another step. "I won't tell Dad," she said softly.

Don't touch me, he prayed. Don't put your hand on my shoulder, don't put your hand on my hair. He was so close to the brink that all it would take was that one gesture, the touch of family, to send him sliding.

His face was turned away from her, but Summer felt the warning, and something leapt inside her. For a moment she just watched the lights from the television flicker on her brother's hair.

She was wondering about A.J., where he'd gone that night, what he'd seen.

· SEVEN ·

A.J. AWOKE IN the dark, before the alarm. He felt like a stone at the bottom of a deep pool. When his eyes focused on the familiar shapes of his bureau and desk, relief swelled under his ribs.

He glanced at the clock. The luminous green numbers read 4:28. He knew it would ring at any moment; he had hockey practice this morning, before school. Reluctantly he pulled his arm out from under the warm quilt and clapped down on the button.

The pain almost made him cry out. For a moment he just lay curled up on his side, gasping. But he had to see.

He staggered out of bed and pushed up the light switch with his forearm. Just looking made him wince.

The asphalt had turned his palms to bloody burlap, and his fingers were swollen and stiff.

He lifted his head then and caught his reflection in the small mirror that hung beside the bureau. He had to look twice. He didn't know that face, the color of an old sheet, blue hollows under the eyes. His right shoulder ached—he was sure something had stretched—and the pounding in his head was worse than any hangover. He felt like he'd been on the losing end of a drunken brawl.

He leaned back, the wall cold against his naked shoulders. The picture was burning a hole in his head, and the word came speeding at him, vicious, whiplike. But he caught it before contact.

It's a joke, A.J., a joke. Come on. Where's your sense of humor? You know him. You know him like yourself. God, he's such a goof. Crazy Tul.

And beneath the words in his head, like the unseen tug of the tide, was the feeling. *It isn't, because it can't be.*

A.J. pushed himself away from the wall and began looking for his clothes.

By five o'clock he was on his way down the stairs. When he heard the clatter of dishes in the kitchen, it made him pause. Of course his father was up—he had to be at the dairy by six—but it had slipped the boy's mind somehow. A.J. didn't want to see anyone; he didn't want to have to talk. And underneath his determined exterior was the small, irrational fear that the night still showed on him, like a bruise.

In the kitchen he turned abruptly towards the counter.

"Hi, Dad," he mumbled. He poured steaming coffee into a mug, trying to use only his fingertips, which hurt the least.

Decco Brandiosa was leaning against the other counter, right in front of the sink. Mornings were kind to him. Sleep had smoothed away some of the creases, and he looked younger, trimmer, in his lawn-green uniform.

"You were late last night," he said.

A.J. swallowed and kept moving. Gingerly he pulled bread out of the bag and dropped two slices into the toaster.

"I know," he said.

"I wanted you to help me move the couch back."

"I know. I'm sorry," A.J. said shortly. "We'll do it to-night."

"Tonight is too late. I needed you last night."

"Well, let's move the damn thing *now,* then!" A.J. jerked around irritably.

Decco stared, unmoving, but his eyes narrowed.

"What happened to you?" he asked.

The question gave the boy an uncomfortable start, but then he realized his father was talking about his hands. A.J. turned back to the counter.

"I fell off my bike."

"Were you hit?"

"No . . ."

"Were you drinking?"

"Jesus Christ!" A.J. slammed the butter knife down on the counter. "Is that all you ever think about? I was side-swiped, okay? By a car, okay? I'm sorry—I didn't get his phone number so you could call and check it out. I will next time, okay?"

A.J. caught himself. Oh, God, what was he yelling for? He almost never yelled, almost never raised his voice, not here in the house. He held his breath.

But his father just stared at him intently, and said, "There's Mercurochrome in the medicine cabinet. And gauze."

A.J. heard the click of the toaster, and it gave him an

excuse to turn away. For a moment the only sound was the scraping of his knife over the bread.

"It's okay," he said at last. "I used some already." And then, "I'm sorry."

His father didn't reply but the silence wasn't angry, it was expectant. He's waiting for me to tell him, the boy realized. The courtesy was as unexpected as a hug. A.J. sat at the table, forcing down the toast and thinking again how different this last month had been. He was wondering if maybe sometime they really could talk.

Decco had his coat on now and was collecting his lunch from the fridge. He stopped and looked out the window.

"Tully's here," he said, "with the car."

A.J.'s stomach lurched. He wasn't ready for this. He didn't have it all planned out in his head yet, what to say and how to act.

"Better hustle," Decco said. "He's on his way up the walk."

That did it. A.J. leapt out of his chair and grabbed his jacket. He was suddenly frightened of letting Tully into the house. He couldn't meet his eyes, not here in the kitchen in front of his father.

A.J. scooped up his hockey equipment, grimacing as he slung his skates over the hurt shoulder.

"I won't be home for supper," Decco said. "Get something for yourself, okay?"

"See you later," A.J. murmured, and then he was through the door, pushing past Tully, who was just coming up the steps.

"Hi, thanks for the ride, let's go," A.J. said, the words all rushing together. He didn't look up.

By the time Tully crawled in behind the steering wheel,

A.J. was already slouched in the passenger seat, half-hidden by the duffel bag on his knees. The blond boy snapped the Mustang into first gear, spraying loose gravel.

At first there was no sound except the engine and the radio. A.J. concentrated on staring out his side window, unconsciously clutching his skates and bag, as if he expected someone to grab for them. At a stoplight, Tully let go of the steering wheel and reached behind his seat.

"Here," he said, dropping the biking gloves on top of A.J.'s bag. "You left them at Chicco's."

A.J. felt a small puncture at the mention of the pool hall but he was grateful for some kind of words to fill the silence.

"Oh, yeah," he said, looking at his palms. "Better late than never."

Tully stared. "Holy mother, what happened to you?" he asked, leaning closer for a better look. A.J. flinched, a reflex, but so obvious that he could have kicked himself.

"Can you believe it?" He laughed nervously. "Evel Knievel got sideswiped on his bike."

"You've gotta stop racing those eighteen wheelers," Tully said, grinning half-heartedly. "They're sore losers."

Conversation sat like a boulder in front of them, but they tried to push it along. They talked about biking and hockey and the game that night, grasping for anything safe. When A.J. listened to himself, it was like listening to a stranger. He was distant and formal, and so polite. He barely knew what he was saying, because his mind was racing ahead, planning what to say next.

Keep it moving, he thought. Just get through this. Get through this and you'll be okay.

When they pulled into the parking lot, A.J. could feel

how early it was. There were hardly any cars and in front of the paling sky, the arena loomed. To A.J. it looked like an island. There were people in there, and something to do. He knew he couldn't hold on here much longer.

As soon as the engine was off, A.J. moved to get out. But Tully sat like a statue, the keys in his hand.

"Wait a minute," he said. A.J. caught his breath, but he paused, his eyes locked on the door handle he was gripping, in pain.

"Let's cut the bullshit, okay?" Tully said softly. "I was up all night thinking about this. Last night . . . was an accident. I never meant for you to find out like that. But I guess, I'm, you know, relieved because I was going—"

"Don't." A.J. cut him off, his nerves twitching. "Don't tell me anything, Tul. I don't want to know."

"Look—do you think this is easy?"

"Shut up, Tully!" A.J.'s voice strained and snapped. He pushed his way out and stumbled into the parking lot. He leapt towards the arena in a blind rush, the car door hanging open behind him.

Coach Landau was pleased. He leaned against the boards beside the bench, and bit the inside of his cheek to keep from smiling. Smiling was black luck for a coach, and doubly worse now, so early in the season. But the feeling was there. It was a team studded with promises.

Al Weitzammer was one of them. He had the softest hands Landau had ever seen. Weitzammer caught a pass with a butterfly net, not a stick. And precise. Never mind picking corners for shots. You could divide the goal into thirty-two squares and the boy would take out the one you asked for. Landau knew this was Weitzammer's last year before he was scooped for Junior, but it didn't matter. He would use him while he had him.

And there were others, less obvious, maybe. Landau skimmed over them with his eyes, checking them off mentally. Lavalle and Pilka were good together. Landau could see a rhythm developing, a one-two passing punch when it worked. McEwan and Zarich were coming close, too, and Gord Rudachuk was a devil of a mucker. No blistering hotshot on open ice, but could he go to the corners! He was a worker, as tenacious as a bulldog, and about as smart. Landau liked Rudachuk.

Millyard, Brown; Landau nodded unconsciously. His gaze caught on A.J. Brandiosa, and he watched. And watched.

Jeez, he's a mess today, the coach thought. He'd been cautiously hopeful about the husky defense. Brandiosa was solidly entrenched in bulldozer hockey, but every now and then Landau had seen glimmers of something better. A.J. could focus and he could react. When he did, the hit or play was naturally smooth, dead on. It was the kind of instinct that could make a coach's heart beat fast.

But it wasn't there today. Today the boy looked like a marionette cursed to a bad puppeteer. When he moved, he jerked and flopped, but too often he was motionless, drifting.

He's asleep or he's stoned, Landau thought.

A.J. wasn't asleep, he was falling. He kept clutching his stick, hoping that the fresh pain in his hands would prop him up.

And he talked to himself. It was only a scrimmage, but he followed the play inside his head, like a sportscaster. The words crowded him. He needed to be crowded.

. . . Rudachuk in the corner, gets it out, Rudachuk to Pilka, Pilka's looking for Lavalle, over the blue line, still looking, pass to Mendel . . .

Oh, God.

. . . back to Pilka, who goes straight into the boards! Good check by Zarich! Scooped up by Millyard, who takes it over center ice. Pass to Weitzammer, to Millyard, to Weitzammer . . .

In his house. In his car. But he never touched me. I swear it. I swear to God.

. . . tied up at the boards. Play is whistled dead. Weitzammer and Grummett at the face-off, Weitzammer has it—shoots!—off the goal post. Caught up by Rudachuk, who takes it behind the net. He's looking, looking, Rudachuk passes to Grummett . . .

That's it. He's gone. Cut him loose, the queer bastard! He's lucky I don't kill him.

. . . Grummett at center ice, Weitzammer trying to intercept, he's on him, he's on . . .

Three years. How didn't I know? I *should've* known. But he didn't touch me, I swear—

And Bill Grummett slid past A.J. to within kissing distance of the goalie and neatly flicked the puck into the right-hand corner of the net.

There was no crowd, but Grummett did his victory dance anyway. A.J.'s side of the rink let out a collective sigh of disgust. Mendel sidled past the defenseman and jogged his shoulder, not nicely.

"Are you nailed to the freakin' ice? Wake up—or get the hell off!"

A.J. turned abruptly and headed for the boards, his face on fire. He wanted to crawl onto the bench and hide, but Landau was in the way.

"I don't know who that was," the coach said, "but you tell him to quit borrowing your jersey."

He flipped the words at A.J. lightly, but his face was taut. It was a warning.

A.J. spun around and started for the locker room. He could almost feel Landau's glare burning his back. He knew this was insolent and insubordinate, but he was past caring.

Inside he stripped off his uniform mechanically and padded across the floor, a towel wrapped around his hips. The empty room was too quiet, unnatural. He was desperate to be gone. But just before the showers, he stopped.

The posting was still up—Landau's final roster for the team—no one had ever taken it off the wall. A.J. stood, a tingle crawling over his scalp, unable to keep his eyes from sliding down over the numbers to the name.

19—Derek Lavalle.

It was not a name he knew. Derek Lavalle didn't go to Riverview. A.J. couldn't ever remember playing on any teams with him. He kept reading it over and over, hypnotized by the black letters on the white paper, as if that would explain something. Maybe why. Maybe how.

Until he realized what he was doing. A.J. recoiled and fled for the showers. He cranked up the temperature and scrubbed himself until his skin was stinging. It's over, A.J., he told himself. You don't care why, you don't ever want to know how. It doesn't matter.

Except for the thought that dug into his heart like a splinter. For three years I told him everything, and he didn't tell me this.

· EIGHT ·

"WELL, WELL. MEET my son, Sleeping Beauty."

There was a giggle. A.J. could only hear with one ear, but it was undeniably a giggle. A female sound. In *this* house?

His eyelashes brushed upholstery. He'd fallen asleep on the couch, his face pressed into the crevice behind the cushions. He rolled over and pushed himself up on his elbows, blinking.

"How nice. It's alive," the giggler said.

It *was* a woman, a small woman in a man's warm-up jacket; the sleeves came to her knuckles. She had frizzy mouse-brown hair and cheeks as round and smooth as Gravensteins. Standing beside her, all dark hollows and leather lines, Decco looked a hundred years old.

A.J. sat up. Who was this? What was she doing here in the living room with his father?

"What time is it?" he croaked, his voice hoarse with sleep.

"Around seven," Decco said.

A.J. jumped. He had to be on the ice in half an hour. He swung his feet over the side of the couch and tried to leave, but his father stopped him with his eyes.

"June, this is A.J. A.J., this is June."

A.J. stood up, swaying slightly. His hand enveloped hers. He could have crushed it, it was so small. A child's hand.

Out of the corner of his eye, he saw his father beaming at the both of them.

"Gotta go," he mumbled. "Game."

In the bathroom, his mind stumbled forward. Who was this June? Why was she here? They had guests so seldom; occasional relatives or someone from the dairy, and Tully. The thought snapped at him but he shrank from it, before the bite.

June. Setup city? he wondered, splashing water on his face. Once or twice his father had introduced him to the daughters of his coworkers, at company barbecues and such. But this June was too old for him. She was in her twenties, at least.

There wasn't time to puzzle it through, not now. By the time he hit the hallway he was flying. Shoes. Jacket. Gear. He was going to sneak out through the kitchen, but he felt a tug of conscience. Better say good-bye, he thought, and leaned into the living-room doorway.

They were on the couch, watching TV. Holding hands. A.J. stepped back, as if from a cliff edge. He backed up through the kitchen, conscious of every breath, every rustle. Then he was through the door, his cheeks burning in the dark night air.

So that's what she was. She was a date. Or something.

His father had had dates before. Nice ladies with square-heeled shoes and tiny lines around their eyes. The kind of ladies you called ma'am.

A.J. felt sick. That person on the couch was a kid. He calculated quickly. Even if she was twenty-five, she was young enough to be his own sister.

What could she possibly see in him? What did his father want from her? Sex. The word ricocheted loudly inside A.J.'s head, and he flinched, as if someone had shouted it on the street. But he was alone. For the first time Tully's absence was palpable, as if someone had punched a hole in the air beside him.

A.J. realized he had slowed to a shuffle. He wanted to lie down and go back to sleep. He wanted to bury his face in the grass and have it all be better when he got up.

He started to jog awkwardly, the duffel bag banging into his calf with every step. He couldn't risk another performance on the ice like this morning's practice. He had to push everything out of his head and plow through this game somehow. Alone.

Bad timing, Tul, A.J. thought, narrowing his eyes against the wind that watered them. Bad freaking timing.

The dressing room hummed with high-voltage energy.

"All right," Landau said, pacing a little as he prepared to brief them. "There's not much to tell. The Terriers are 1 and 4 for the year."

"The *Terriers*?" Grant Pilka muttered incredulously.

"Arf, arf!" a voice barked, and everyone laughed. A.J.'s jaw tightened. He knew it was Tully at the back of the room.

Even Landau grinned. "Right. The Terriers. They

haven't had much of a year, but don't get cocky. Bruce Fleury is back."

"Out on bail!" Bill Grummett called.

"No kidding? What's the charge?"

"He murdered three wingers in O.T.," Tully cried over the din. "You know . . ."

"Sudden death overtime!" the room chorused.

Landau threw his pencil up and let it fall. He'd get no sense out of them tonight. He called orders as they filed out of the dressing room, but the words were lost in the exuberant noise. As A.J. passed, he reached out and patted the boy's shoulder, just below the bulky pad. It was fatherly, forgiving. It was a gift.

A.J. didn't pause, didn't even raise his eyes, but the feeling rippled through him. Here in this place, with these guys, he was part of something. It was the first time he'd felt human in twenty-four hours.

Stumping off the ice after warm-ups, Grant Pilka whistled under his breath. "Jesus, Mary and Joseph," he said.

"If we had 'em, I'd play 'em," Weitzammer muttered, his mood uncharacteristically dark. But there was no mistaking what they were seeing.

These guys are in the wrong sport, A.J. thought, his eyes on the ice. Linebackers—every last one of them.

It wasn't completely true. The infamous Bruce Fleury was tall enough, but raw-looking, unfed. A handful of others were distinctly average-sized. But the rest, perhaps two strings' worth, looked like rectangles on skates.

"No sweat," A.J. said, pushing the words purposefully out of his mouth. "We'll clean up the boards with 'em."

"Easy for you to say, Brandiosa." Pilka shook his head. "Looks like a passing game to me."

"All right," Weitzammer said, scrambling to rally them. "Let's run the S.O.B.'s into the ground. Play your partners. There's no way they'll keep up to us—no way!"

But he was wrong. Bruce Fleury and the first string lit out of their zone as if the ice were tilted. It wasn't that they were fast—Weitzammer had been right about that— they were just coordinated. Partners. The defensemen had the intuition of twins.

Still on the bench, A.J. watched through narrow eyes, trying not to let the others see the awe in his face. Lately in practice, he'd been working with Trent Millyard, and he'd felt pretty good about the patterns they'd run together.

Amateurs, he thought now, his throat closing up. We are freaking amateurs.

And then the line changed and Rod Mendel puffed through the gate, and amateur number 27 leapt up as if someone had booted him.

A.J. was determined not to back down. He was sure that once he had a few hits under his belt, he'd settle, and this game would be like any other. But it was difficult. No one player seemed to carry the puck long enough to make contact.

They were superb headmanners. When the puck was in their own zone, the carrier didn't shuffle behind the net, looking for a hero's path out. The puck went zinging ahead to the next player, then up to the next—bang, bang, bang—until it was deep in the Cyclone end. And there it was delivered to Bruce Fleury. In the first period Fleury squared off against goalie Terry Frances half a dozen times. He nailed it in twice.

It's the second goal that panics you, A.J. thought. The first riles you, the prick of a needle. A second goal drives it in with a slam and you jump, even before the pain registers, because you know if you don't do something, it's going to hurt.

A.J. jumped. It was on a rebound, deflected off the goalie's stick in the Cyclones' end. When he had it, Pilka's good advice about a passing game evaporated.

Go, damn it, go! his mind screamed, and he took off, although he was behind his own blue line and players teemed at center ice like sharks.

It was a panic charge, a flat-out, two-points-behind run along the boards, and he never should have tried it. Millyard had elbowed out past his guard and was shouting for a pass. He was hardly a blur in A.J.'s right eye.

A.J. was focusing. The whole rink had become a patch against the far boards, three feet square, that he had nailed his eyes to. Just get there, his heart drummed, get to the boards and swing around the net. Someone will be there. You'll get the assist.

And while that thought was still sweet in his mind, he heard the cry, the warning. He never knew where it came from. He only had time to move his head a quarter turn before he slammed into the boards.

There are hits, and there are hits. A check twelve inches into the boards that you half expect isn't nice, but it isn't awful. A.J. had flown three feet, bounced and then slammed back into the shoulder that had hit him.

There was a ripple of a cheer when he raised himself to his feet on the arm of a linesman; it was a home game. But A.J. slunk to the box. It had been a bad hit, but legal.

He averted his eyes as he shuffled to a seat.

"Go get Vic to look at you," Landau said. "You may need to have your ribs taped."

"After the period," A.J. said, because he couldn't bear the thought of crawling away in front of everyone. He glared at the rink, wincing with every breath, the words chugging like a train in his head. Stupid, stupid, stupid . . .

In the dying minutes of the period, the play was locked in the home end. The Terriers had the Cyclones well covered. Rudachuk skittered behind the net, trapped.

Then, an opening. From the bench, A.J. could see the path as if it were painted on the ice. He was on the edge of his seat.

"Go, Gordy," A.J. muttered.

Rudachuk saw the opening, too. He whipped around the right-hand side of the net, then hesitated.

A.J. was wringing his stick. The opening was there! For Christ's sake, rush it, Gord!

But Rudachuk choked. He shot blindly towards the point, a broad pass in Weitzammer's direction. It never connected. The Terrier line had just changed, and a fresh Fleury streaked forward, intercepted, and effortlessly snapped it into the net.

The moan seemed to come out of the arena's beams, like a shudder. Mendel swore so loudly he startled parents six rows up. A.J. closed his eyes. This wasn't a beating, it was a one-man war.

The period ended mercifully soon, and the Cyclones trudged off, dark-eyed with disgust. But no one said anything to Gord. Rudachuk was the kind of guy who tried so hard, all the time. He did the dirty work. He scuffled and scrambled and dug, without complaint. He was a beautiful mucker, so you had to let the other errors go.

But Gord wasn't letting it go. When he pushed, ashen-faced, into the locker room, A.J. knew the boy was carrying Fleury's hat trick by himself.

A.J. waited in a secluded corner of the room, wincing under the brusque once-over by Vic, the trainer. After the pronouncement—bruised—he sat, slouched on the bench. Without the diversion of the game, the night seemed to fold in on him, suffocating. He saw Rudachuk shuffle over to the drinking fountain, his shoulders bowed.

And then, "Hey, Gord. Good play."

"Huh?" Rudachuk looked up, a flinch, as if he expected to be struck.

"I said, good play." Lavalle had pulled off his helmet and was toweling some of the sweat out of his hair. He grinned.

A.J. stared, frozen. For twenty-four hours Lavalle had been a faceless figure, hovering darkly at the edge of his vision. Now he couldn't look at anything else.

Rudachuk was bewildered. The Terriers had just scored off his mindless pass. There was nothing good about the play. But Lavalle's expression was open, engaging.

Number 19 draped the towel over his shoulder and stepped closer.

"I could see what you were setting up for, and it was brilliant. I mean, everybody was in perfect position. You at the net, Weitzammer at the point . . ."

Rudachuk was listening intently, the disbelief kindling into half hope. Lavalle was so convincing that even A.J. began rebuilding the scene in his head, wondering for the first time if it *had* been a great play that had gone awry.

Or is he trying to be nice, make Gord feel better, A.J. thought. He knew nothing about this guy, or what made him tick.

". . . and Pilka was open, just waiting to tip it into their net. It was a *beautiful* setup"—Lavalle was almost whispering into Rudachuk's face—"that only a brain-damaged *choke* would ever try."

Rudachuk straightened, his face white. Someone else might have sworn at Lavalle, or hammered him into the lockers, but that just wasn't Gord, not even when he was bleeding. Lavalle was able to saunter away, unscathed.

A.J. hadn't moved from his spot on the bench. But inside, the wheels were whirring.

So that's what you are, he thought. Even inside his head the words were icy. He had known nothing about Lavalle, and now he knew a great deal. He had a label, another one. Manipulator.

"All right, all right, quit your bellyaching." Landau's voice rose over the din. "Let's see what the hell we can do about it."

It was a vivid lecture, short and not sweet at all. They weren't playing the game they were good at. They were letting the Terriers rattle them. Under pressure, Landau was not a coach who gently coaxed and inspired. He was a ballbreaker.

When it was over, the guys slunk away to wait for the whistle that would start the second period. A.J. pulled himself up wearily and stopped. Landau was standing in front of him.

"How are your ribs?" he asked.

A.J. took a breath, testing. "Okay. Vic says I'm probably bruised." He hurried to cover any cracks of doubt. "But I can play. I feel really good."

The coach nodded absently. He had a toothpick in his mouth and moved it from one side to the other. The noise level was rising, everybody gearing up to face the ice again.

"I think it's time you asked Mr. Fleury for a date," Landau said quietly.

"What?" A.J. drew himself up. His head was so full of dark images that he could only interpret one way.

Landau looked directly into A.J.'s eyes.

"You're a big boy," the coach said slowly, deliberately. "I think you should go on a date with Mr. Fleury." There was a second's pause. "And ask him about his poor left knee."

A.J. blinked. Fleury? Date?

Take him out. The answer thunked A.J. in the back of the head like a stray stick. Take him out of the game.

He looked up again, but all he saw was Landau's back moving through the crowd to the door.

· NINE ·

IT WAS MONDAY morning. At his school locker, A.J. shuffled through his books, trying to assemble what he needed for his first classes.

"Hey, Bad Boy!"

The words zinged down the hallway, but A.J. didn't look up.

"Yeah, Brandiosa. Bad Boy!", This time he did look, bewildered. Harold Doerkson loped up and slapped him solidly on the arm.

"Who would have thunk it!" Doerkson chortled happily. "Brandiosa, you don't look the type. But all I knows is what I reads in the papers."

Half of A.J.'s mouth turned up in a guarded grin. He had no idea what Doerkson was babbling about.

Then someone shoved A.J. from behind, playfully. He whirled around. Glen Rasmussen backed up in mock horror.

"Ooh, quick on the draw. Don't hurt me, Bad Boy."

A.J. flushed crimson. He didn't know whether to get mad or shrug it off. What was going on?

Doerkson sighed. It was no fun trying to tease somebody who didn't know it.

"Lloyl," he explained, settling against the blue lockers. "Ted Lloyl, his column? You were hot press on Saturday. What's the matter, you live in a cave or something?"

A.J. felt a small pang. This first weekend alone, he *had* lived in a cave, four walls and his bed.

Then the information began to register. Ted Lloyl was the sportswriter who reported on junior and minor hockey. It wouldn't be considered a big-time column anywhere else, but Moose Jaw, with its near-cult following of the junior leagues, was a different matter. People read Ted Lloyl.

"Have you got one?" A.J. croaked suddenly, his vocal cords surprised to be in use.

Rasmussen looked down deliberately at his own crotch. "Well, it was there this morning."

Doerkson guffawed, pounding the other boy on the back. A.J. grinned tiredly, waiting for the stupid joke to subside. The first buzzer cut in, blasting them, and the two boys started to troop off, still elbowing each other.

Doerkson turned around, and walking backwards called out, "Check the cafeteria. But you'd better hustle, Bad Boy."

A.J. flew down the hallway to the cafeteria, plunked down his fifty cents, and slid into his Geometry 30 class moments after the second bell. He fidgeted through a fifteen-minute lecture on logarithms before the class settled into its assignment and the teacher, Mr. Pearson, left the room.

A.J. rattled through the newspaper quickly, then folded it so that he could slide it under his textbook. The headline almost leapt off the page at him.

BAD BOY ENDS FLEURY'S SEASON

A.J. blinked, then blinked again. And then he began to read.

The Terriers' exceptional center, Bruce Fleury, was back with a vengeance Friday. Fleury, out with stretched knee ligaments since the second game of the season, was in superb form as the Terriers took on the fifth-ranked Cyclones. By the end of the first, the center had chalked up no less than a hat trick, effectively neutralizing the Cyclones' strong defense. Even the Cyclones' top scorers—Al Weitzammer and Grant Pilka—were pinned by an energized Terrier front line.

And then it all came apart. Midway through a scoreless second period, Fleury was assaulted by the heretofore also-ran of a defense, A.J. Brandiosa. Don't be misled—this wasn't a check. This wasn't even a normal display of temper. This was a calculated running dive targeted for the side of Fleury's left leg. And it hit the mark.

The Cyclones paid—Brandiosa was penalized with a five-minute major plus a match suspension—but Fleury paid a higher price. The shining center is out for another six-week stretch, possibly longer.

A.J.'s fingers were blurring the newsprint. He remembered with frightening clarity the sensation of Fleury's leg buckling.

A.J. skimmed over the next part of the article because he

knew the plot—how the Cyclones rallied to kill the penalty, how the Terriers lost their focus without Fleury. Weitzammer's two goals; Pilka and Brown one apiece.

He was just pushing the newspaper back under his book when his eyes caught on the tail of Lloyl's column.

No one will argue that Junior is a particularly physical brand of hockey. Maybe these kids think they have to prove themselves. But the hit Fleury took Friday night wasn't physical, it was brutal.

This is Brandiosa's first year in Triple A. If the burly 16-year-old is bucking to establish himself as the league Bad Boy, he's got my vote.

A.J. sat, the words fading to fuzz in front of him. He could still see Fleury vividly, how small his sweat-soaked head had seemed when they tore the helmet off him. How light he looked when they lifted him up. He wasn't a big kid. A.J. could have carried Fleury alone.

I never meant to hurt him, A.J. reasoned silently. But he knew it was a lie. At that moment on the ice, he had meant to hurt Bruce Fleury. Take him out. And it had been so easy; despising Derek Lavalle, still reeling over Tully, mad as hell at himself for his own stupidity. It had been so easy it frightened him.

Bad Boy. The memory of Doerkson's voice ringing down the hall made A.J. cringe. He wasn't a goon. Attacking Fleury hadn't even been his idea. But shifting blame was a crutch.

So just take it, he thought. It's like a penalty. Take it and keep your mouth shut and pretty soon Fleury will be back on the ice and everyone will forget. You'll get another shot at making good.

He picked up his pencil and determinedly started scratching out the first equations. But he couldn't keep from wondering, just briefly, if Tully ever read Ted Lloyl.

It seemed that everyone else in Riverview Collegiate did. A.J.'s new title was handed around like a torch. He heard it again and again—in the hallways, in class, going for lunch. At first he was defensive, then he was bewildered. Sympathy for Bruce Fleury was nonexistent. The center lived across town, but it might as well have been the other side of the world.

The kids at Riverview Collegiate liked A.J.'s notoriety, and the idea of having an antihero in their midst. It was excitement, it was news.

In the cafeteria at noon, A.J. found himself securely knit into the fabric of the crowd. The group seemed to gather at his table. He had been dreading the lunch hours. He and Tully always went somewhere to eat, or just cruised downtown in the Mustang. The empty hour had worried him; he lived too far away to walk home. He didn't know how to eat alone in a crowded school.

But he wasn't alone now. The table ate and drank the game. A.J. was sitting beside Paul Treejack, a big-boned kid with shoulder-length, heavy-metal hair. Treejack was tearing apart last night's game period by period. He was a big kid, but ungainly; A.J. knew Treejack didn't have the coordination to make it around one of Landau's pylon courses. Funny how the guys who didn't play were all pros.

"Hey, listen. Fleury's been begging for it for a long

time," Paul Treejack said, his forearm flexing as he sopped up gravy. "Every hotshot's the same. He'll fancy dance with the puck, but you show him a little elbow, and he's cryin' to the ref. Or worse, he's flying the other way." Treejack bit off half his dinner roll and chewed vigorously. "Fleury can shoot all right, but he's got faggot skates."

The group burst into sudden laughter. A.J. started; the word was a whip. But self-preservation gripped him quickly and he laughed along with them.

Table talk deteriorated then, into a cheerful discussion of faggot skates. Who had them and who didn't. How you had to be careful because if you ever bought second-hand equipment, you might get a pair.

"And then you're contaminated," Paul Treejack said. He leaned back and grinned wickedly. "You can get your stick up, all right, you just can't score."

They all groaned. The whole lunch hour had been stupid and raunchy and blustery and the safest hour of the whole day. When the bell finally sounded, A.J. was reluctant to leave.

"See you 'round," he said, turning abruptly so that it would look like it didn't matter.

Then, on cue, the whole table sang out, "See you, Bad Boy!" He walked out of the cafeteria a lot taller than he had walked in. At least he wasn't total human wreckage. Maybe slamming Fleury wasn't right, but nobody seemed to think it was wrong.

Farther down, he felt a more specific relief. Doerkson and Treejack were good guys to be on friendly terms with. At Riverview, Treejack especially held a lot of sway. A.J. knew he might need that approval sometime.

Insurance, he thought. For the day he couldn't bear to

think about—the day somebody else found out about Tulsa Brown and the dirt flew that A.J. Brandiosa had been friends with a queer. Or worse.

By 3:30 he felt safer, more settled. His ego had been padded all afternoon. He began to think that no matter what happened, he could ride it out.

Get out more, he told himself as he dumped his books in his locker. See more people. Date somebody, for Pete's sake, and you'll be okay.

Somebody was waiting for him on the school steps. Still paces from the door, A.J. stopped. His first impulse was to turn and hurry out another door.

But she saw him. She didn't have to wave. Her hazel eyes locked into his and he was trapped.

A.J. began walking again, more slowly, but still forward. Blank, he thought. Just make your face blank.

"Hi," he said.

"If you think I'm here to congratulate you on your big press break, you're nuts," Summer said. "The vicious streak of infantile violence that is inherent to your sex does not impress me."

"It's nice to see you, too," A.J. said.

Her cheeks turned the faintest pink. "Okay. Hi. How are you."

"Fine," A.J. said.

"How's your dad."

A.J. felt a twinge. "Fine."

"Now I'd like to talk to you. Please," she added. The boy fell into step with her as she began to walk through the schoolyard. The overcast sky, a solid sheet of white turning gray, seemed low enough to press them to the ground.

"How was your ride the other night?" Summer asked.

He'd known it was coming to this. "It was all right," A.J. said woodenly. "A bit cold."

"I waited all weekend for you to call me. You said you'd tell me. You *promised*." He kept walking, staring at the frost-bitten ground.

"There wasn't anything I could tell you," he said. That wasn't a lie.

Summer was persistent. She knew how small Moose Jaw was. "You didn't find him?"

"No."

"You didn't even see his car somewhere?"

A.J. threw up his hands. "Look, I'm not his keeper, all right? He's your brother, not mine. You want to know where he goes—ask him!"

They walked in silence until they reached the gate into the schoolyard. He would turn right to walk home; she would turn left towards her bus stop.

Summer leaned against the chain-link fence. "You could have called just to say hello," she said, staring at the traffic. "I mean, we don't see a lot of you anymore. For three years you're around the house like the wallpaper, and then you're not around at all."

A.J. was dumbfounded. Was she trying to say she missed him?

Summer shrugged and laughed nervously. "We keep setting the table for five."

"Why don't you come out to a game sometime?" he blurted.

Her mouth twisted. "Get serious. I hate hockey."

His thoughts were racing. *Don't do this, A.J. It can't ever work—not now.* But he said, "It's not so bad. I could meet you after. We could talk or something."

Summer shrugged again. "Maybe. Sometime."

It was vague, but the words settled inside him, as warm as hot chocolate. Why was it like this with her? How could she make him feel defensive and protective and hopeful, all in the same conversation?

"My bus'll be coming in a minute," she said, pushing off the fence. "I have to go."

"See you," A.J. said.

Summer glanced up, but then she stopped and her face broke into a surprised, unabashed smile. She pointed at him. A.J. craned his neck to see.

The first fragile snowflake of the year was sitting on his shoulder.

By the time he got home, the powder was swirling around him dizzily. Visibility was bad, but not altogether gone. A.J. didn't miss the big brown pickup truck parked in the driveway. His buoyant mood clunked back to earth. *She* was here, again.

The subject of June had not come up with his father. On Friday night, when A.J. had arrived home from the game, she had been gone.

Maybe it was just a one-time thing, A.J. had thought, but he knew he was rationalizing. He just hadn't been ready for a confrontation, not that night.

But tonight was different. A.J. opened the door and went inside.

They were in the kitchen together, cooking something. Through the doorway he could see them puttering around.

Passing Decco, June touched his arm, a familiar, absent-minded touch that sent a shot running through A.J.'s chest. She's so goddamned at ease, the boy thought. So goddamned at home. He stamped the snow off his runners loudly.

"So—you're home," Decco called. He wandered out of the kitchen wearing the chef's apron A.J. had given him one Christmas. It was a funny apron, vertical blue and white stripes that would have made someone else look comical. But Decco never looked comical.

A.J. leaned against the wall, still in his jacket, the snow melting on his sneakers. He let the accusation glimmer in his eyes.

Decco meandered towards him. "Take off your coat and stay awhile," he said. He was smiling, but the words were not flippant; they were a warning.

"I don't know if I'm staying," A.J. said. He had absolutely nowhere to go, but his father couldn't know that. "I wouldn't want to break up anything *cozy*. You know, three's a crowd?"

Decco was closer now. They were standing in the same hallway, the same dangerous air space. The muscles in the man's cheek twitched.

"Grow up," he said flatly. "You're acting like a ten-year-old."

"Just about your speed, hey, Dad? Grown-up women are too smart, but it's not hard to pull the strings on some *kid.*"

"That's enough." Decco caught the boy's arm.

"No, it isn't enough!" A.J.'s eyes were glittering. "You go ahead and have your midlife crisis or whatever, but don't parade it in front of me. My God, you should be embarrassed—"

"The sauce is ready," June interrupted, appearing suddenly in the kitchen doorway. She was holding a wooden spoon and staring at them with the most even, unruffled gaze. "Are you two going to fight or eat?"

In the awkward silence, Decco let go his grip and A.J. felt his own rush of temper deflate. But it didn't disappear.

"I'm not hungry," he muttered, turning away from them and moving blindly up the stairs.

In fifteen minutes he was sorry. Not because he wanted to be downstairs; God, just listening to the sound of them made him ill. The occasional bang of pots, the faint rattle of cutlery. Once he heard Decco laugh, and his skin almost crawled off his bones.

Of course the worst sound was no sound—long stretches of ten or twelve seconds when he could vividly imagine them pressed together in the kitchen or the dining room.

There was a softball on the dresser, left over from summer. He began to toss it lightly into the air, but the ceiling was far too low for any kind of a throw. The ball didn't even sting his hands.

A.J. lay back on the floor beside his bed and began throwing, straight up. For a little while he was absorbed in learning how to pitch so that the ball wouldn't arc foward or backward out of his reach.

Once he had it mastered, though, the aim and the rhythm, he was craving again. He watched the ball go zinging towards the ceiling, seem to pause, then fall back into his waiting hand. It was hypnotic, but not nearly enough.

He could feel the people below him—the vibration of their footsteps and voices—with his shoulder blades. He clenched his teeth.

He wanted a hard skating drill. Manmakers, even. Open ice and a reason to run that would turn his lungs to fire and wring the muscles in his legs like rags. Or something more.

A hundred pounds. He wanted to be benchpressing a hundred pounds. Fast at first, then slowing to a robotlike pace until the bar was so heavy it felt like someone was pushing back. But not stopping. Staring up at the ceiling, just like now, his shoulder sockets screaming and his stomach muscles tight enough to snap, sweat dribbling into his ears, the whole world sitting on that bar and the dim basement starting to sway, thinking, oh, God . . . I can't . . . not again . . .

"Come on, A.J.! Ten more. You can do it!"

He jerked, and the softball flipped awkwardly out of his hand. It hit the bureau, then bounced once or twice before it rolled to the wall.

A.J. sat up, his heart pounding. His eyes were fastened on the door. It couldn't be, he wouldn't dare. . . . Moments passed and the door stayed shut. The creaky stairway was silent.

A.J. lay shakily back on the floor again, and draped his arm across his eyes. They burned. His whole body burned, as if he really had been fighting under a hundred pounds of iron.

Get away from me, he pleaded with the ghost. Get the hell away from me.

· TEN ·

A.J. KNEW HE had to get the weights back as quickly and painlessly as possible. Every time he closed his eyes he could see them—the bench, the bar, the plates, the bells— sitting silently in Tully's house, gleaming the way a murder weapon must gleam. He had to have them back, in his own house, safe.

He decided to leave a note, one of those little yellow things with adhesive on the back, stuck to Tully's locker. It would be short—"I need my weights" or something—and he wouldn't sign it. He couldn't bear to have his initials hanging on Tully's locker for the whole school to see.

The only problem was how to physically get the set home. The two boys lived six blocks apart, not a comfortable distance to carry two hundred pounds of dead weight.

"Well, he can worry about it," A.J. grumbled to himself. "He's the one with the car."

A.J. scribbled the note Wednesday, then cruised past Tully's locker, waiting for the right moment. On his way to biology class there were too many people milling around. He tried again and again, but the hallways were crowded and he felt self-conscious.

Thursday morning he went to school early, thinking he would get there before the rush. The corridors were almost empty as A.J. turned the corner beside the stairwell. Then he pulled up sharply, his wet runners squeaking on the polished floor.

Tully and Andrea were walking ahead of him, still in their coats. They were probably heading for Tully's locker, but they ambled slowly. Tully had his arm around Andrea's shoulders. The girl's magnificent hair billowed and bowed, caught under his sleeve.

A small pulse of shock skipped through A.J. painfully. Get out of here before he sees you, he ordered himself. But he was rooted to the floor.

Tully turned his head then, leaned towards Andrea and whispered in her ear. She giggled and shoved him with her hip. A.J. didn't have to see her face to know she was blushing. The next moment she was close to Tully again, her thumb hooked in the back belt loop of his jeans.

A.J. backed up; he willed himself to tear his eyes away. When he started to run, his footsteps echoed eerily in the empty halls.

A.J. walked numbly into his homeroom. A few other early students were scattered like islands, reading, studying. There was no danger of anyone talking to him, and he was glad.

He stared at his desk. The image was still crisp in his mind: Tully's arm, Tully's profile, and Andrea. So casual, so normal.

Maybe Tully just made a mistake. Once. Maybe Tully

was confused. A.J. had read that somewhere, that adolescents were sexually confused. That they tried on identities like hats. A.J. couldn't ever remember trying on an identity himself. The one he had was scary enough.

But Tully was such a goof. Game for anything. And he trusted people; the right person at the right time could sell Tully anything.

The first bell sounded and the rest of A.J.'s homeroom class began to wander in. Chairs scraped, desk lids banged, kids bantered back and forth. The noise was around A.J. like a fog.

Saturday afternoon, the Cyclones played the Swift Current Vikings, in Swift Current. A.J. filed off the half-empty bus, stiff-legged and taciturn. Everyone seemed subdued. The uncomfortable two-hour bus ride and overcast sky were enough to dampen anyone's spirits.

Conversation in the dressing room was low, sporadic. No one wanted to open his mouth. In an arena that old, you drew in twenty-five years of salt and sweat with every breath.

A.J. pulled on his pads wearily, shuddering against the initial stiffness. He had no idea how well he would play, didn't know if he felt like playing at all. He'd spent Friday night holed up in his room, his radio turned up to drown out the sound of the television and the people below. June hadn't left until 1:15 A.M. Ignoring someone was exhausting, A.J. thought.

As he was taping his stick, the rest of the team began to arrive. It was the players who had driven from Moose Jaw with their parents, or who simply preferred their own cars. Weitzammer, Kafke, Millyard, Lavalle, Tully and a handful of others burst in just minutes apart, all high spirits and pink cheeks. With the scent of outside still clinging to their clothes, they were literally a breath of fresh air.

"Hey!" Weitzammer called out. "We've got ourselves a cheering section today."

Tully swung his duffel bag onto the bench, grinning. "A whole van full. Bunch of guys from Riverview."

"And girls!" Millyard piped up. "Live ones. Lucious little beauties just dying to lay their hands on . . ."

"Watch it." Tully elbowed him playfully. "My sister's on that van."

". . . our sticks," Millyard finished. The room exploded with laughter.

A.J. felt the eruption inside. Summer had come. With a van full of kids from Riverview. He hadn't heard anything about the expedition being planned, but he could guess who was on it. The thought of Summer being jostled by Treejack or drooled over by Doerkson made his temperature flare. He ate lunch with that crew every day. He knew how sick they were.

He ripped off the white tape and smoothed the edge. It was funny. When he thought about Summer, he didn't picture the few muted conversations they'd had on her front porch. He didn't even see her on the basement stairs. Summer was fixed forever in the dark back seat of the Mustang, highlighted by streetlamps, on the last night the world was right side up.

The noise in the locker room was rising. He tried not to let his eyes rest on Tully. It was like not watching the silver ball in a pinball machine.

Tully, strung out with his usual case of pregame nerves, was everywhere, kidding, prodding. He leapt up onto a bench, half-dressed and barefoot, to air-guitar with his stick. Onlookers whistled and hooted. They loved him. Everybody loved him.

A.J. turned his back to the show and pushed on his helmet, fumbling with the chin strap.

Oh, Tul. If you could just get over it. Back on track. You've gotten out of other things. One mistake doesn't have to screw up your whole life. I'd never bring it up. I swear to God. And I'd be the friend I'm supposed to be. If you could just get over it.

A.J. had underestimated the van from Riverview, and how much noise nine people could make in a small arena. When the Cyclones skated out onto the ice, they were greeted by a thunderblast. Once he heard the cry "Get 'em, Bad Boy!" Treejack.

At this level of hockey, you weren't supposed to notice the crowd, weren't supposed to care. But A.J. soared through warm-ups.

All right, he thought, watching goalie Terry Frances scuff the ice in his crease. All right. Get 'em, Bad Boy.

Swift Current was not a team known for its finesse. The Vikings reminded A.J. of the scrub games that came together in the frozen back lanes—mismatched, uncoordinated and desperately competitive.

It was near the end of the second period, in a game full of abrupt turnarounds and wild dashes down the ice. A.J. knew his team was better than the Vikings; for skating and basic stickhandling, there was no contest.

Then why are we working so hard? he wondered, wiping his mouth on the sleeve of his jersey. The Cyclones'

2–1 edge was precarious. They seemed to be in danger of losing it at any moment.

The answer was easy. Swift Current was a team full of muckers. They weren't neat and they weren't fast, but they dug in and hung on. If the chance came up, they were there. And sometimes they made their own chances. Bill Grummett took an elbow in his windpipe; Grant Pilka was slashed viciously above his ankles.

A.J. was playing hard, trying to shove the Vikings' force back at them. Underneath, he knew he should be concentrating more, trying to move the puck more, being more of a player than a bodyguard.

But nobody's telling me any different, he thought petulantly. Landau hadn't given him any instructions, seemed content with the slam-bang defense. And there was no missing the sudden whoop from the Riverview section every time he took a player down. He would never have admitted how strong that noise made him feel, how it wrapped around and lifted him like an embrace.

As soon as we get a little more ahead, I'll cool down, A.J. told himself. When we secure our edge, I'll start playing right again.

And then at the beginning of the third period, a Viking winger nailed Terry Frances.

It was a stupid, frustrated hit, more like a solid cuff on the side of the head than a blow. But goalies are never prepared to be hit by players, and Terry went down hard.

A.J. was at the blue line when it happened. The unprovoked attack seemed to explode in his vision. The referee whistled the play dead, but A.J. lost his gloves and stick in one quick thrust. Two strides and he had the Viking winger against the boards.

He'd only meant to grab him, shake a little sense into him. But when A.J. took hold of the Viking jersey, the winger threw his arms around him, a bear hug to stall A.J.'s swing. Panic drove through like a white-hot spear.

Don't touch me! his mind shrieked. His arms shot up, breaking the hold, slamming the winger hard into the boards.

"Shithead," the other spat at him. A.J.'s fingers closed around the metal of the player's face cage. He yanked up and the grill snapped off, broken. Then his hand was full of jersey again.

The winger was struggling, trying to protect his face. But A.J. was strong. His heart was thumping and the adrenaline was singing and he knew he could have lifted the winger off the ice. Easy. As easy as curling five pounds, again and again and again. He couldn't stop. Even when his hand came back wet he couldn't stop. He felt the linesmen pulling at him, no more important than leaves falling on his back. The whole world was the rhythm of his arm and the love song descending from the stands.

Tully liked driving at night. He liked the way streetlights slid over the gleaming red hood; he liked the whisper-soft glow of the dash.

On the highway it was even better. He could lose himself in his car on the prairie at night—pretend that he and the Mustang were one metal creature gunning into the darkness.

Tully and Derek were on the highway, driving back from Swift Current. The needle was nudging eighty, on a speedometer that had never heard of metric. Derek was resting his hand on the back of the driver's seat, but he was silent. Tully was relieved. He had a lot to think about.

He was still reeling with the images of the fight. Tully had played hockey with A.J. for three years, and he'd seen him in every mood imaginable. But never like that.

A.J. was a physical defenseman. He could get angry on the ice, angrier than he usually allowed himself, and he could hit hard. He wasn't afraid to mix it up now and then. But not like that. Not ripping off somebody's face mask and pounding and pounding until the blood sprayed. When they'd finally pulled him off, he was still swinging, like a wind-up toy that couldn't run down.

But the frightening part was that he didn't look angry. Tully had expected him to be blistering, red-faced and swearing a blue streak. He wasn't. When A.J. skated off the ice, suspended for the game, he was white. As blank as a tin soldier.

Something's really wrong, was all Tully could think. A.J. was in trouble and he needed help. No one knew better than Tully that A.J. wouldn't ask for it.

Tully gripped the steering wheel tightly, staring at the white lines that blurred on the asphalt. His insides felt like crumpled paper. These past ten days he had forced himself to live in a tunnel; he'd shut his vision down to a very narrow perspective that did not include A.J. Brandiosa. It had kept him from feeling angry, and other things.

Except A.J. was in trouble. Tully was overwhelmed by the intensity of that thought, and how inside his chest it felt, very much, like something else.

"How come you never let me drive?" Derek said suddenly.

The intrusion jarred Tully, then grated on him.

"It's my car. Nobody drives it but me," he said, his eyes never leaving the road.

"Oh, come on." Derek's hand closed in the back of Tully's hair, a loose fist.

"No." Tully tried to shrug him off. "Don't."

"You don't mean it. You never do." The fist tightened; Tully could feel his scalp pull. It was a familiar move, familiar enough to make Tully draw in his breath, but he was determined to fight it. He was not in the mood.

He leaned forward to break contact. Derek yanked him back so hard Tully's shoulders slammed the seat. The Mustang swerved into the oncoming lane, back across the gravel shoulder, before he could right it.

"Jesus Christ!" Tully lashed out blindly with his right hand, an angry reflex. Lightning quick, Derek caught his wrist and pinned it against the backrest.

Tully's heart was shaking his whole body. The grip on his hair was tighter; his chin angled upwards. His arm seemed nailed to the upholstery. Derek was a winger, too. He did all the same exercises to strengthen his wrist shots. Tully struggled to keep his voice even.

"Grow up, Lavalle. You could make me roll this thing."

Hypnotically calm, the words seemed disembodied in the night. "You worship this car, Tulsa. You won't roll it, not if you drive carefully. Besides, you love this. Look at you."

Tully didn't need to look. The speed and darkness and adrenaline had worked on him, despite himself. He was almost touching the steering wheel.

Tully's face burned. This was too far. This was arousal taken over the edge, a sudden, dizzying drop into something else. He was frightened. And yet . . . and yet . . .

"You jerk," he said, his own breath cutting him to a whisper.

"I always drive, Tulsa," Derek said, and he gently released his grip.

"You're home early," Mrs. Brown said, her arms folded over her chest. "The sun isn't up yet."

Tully didn't take the joke. He tried to hang his coat on the closet doorknob. It slid to the floor and lay there. Mrs. Brown followed as Tully wandered towards the kitchen.

"There was no reason Summer couldn't have driven down with you," she said. "Especially if you knew you weren't going to be late. You shouldn't have made her go down with a bunch of kids she doesn't know. That's just plain thoughtless."

Summer was playing solitaire at the kitchen table. She wasn't in a good mood. A.J. had completely ignored her after the game. He'd drifted onto the bus like a zombie while she'd stood there, painfully self-conscious.

"He's afraid to show up with me. I cramp his style, Mom," Summer said acidly, snapping down a card. "All his drug dealer friends think I'm a narc."

But Tully just descended into the basement like a wraith. Summer stared at the black rectangle of the doorway. He hadn't even bothered to turn on the light.

She didn't, either. On the third step from the bottom, she sat down in darkness.

"Don't brood, Tully. Mom and Dad will drag you to their meditation sessions again." She'd meant to flip the words out, but the heavy air caught them like a quilt. The only other sound was the faint sloshing from Tully's waterbed. It needed filling again.

Oh, what's *with* you? she wondered, her hands clenched on top of her lap. Even on drugs he used to talk to her. Not coherently, but he would. She could take him wild, even blistering mad. She could take him cutting her, but not shutting her out.

"Summer," he said. She jumped. The noise seemed to come out of a hollow pit.

"What?"

There was a pause. Summer's short fingernails dug into her knuckles. Then the words started, a soft, strangled torrent.

"Did you ever get into something that wasn't what you expected . . . and it turned out to be better than anything and sometimes worse than anything, and you were scared because . . . because you knew maybe you should get out of it but you didn't think you could?"

For a moment Summer just sat, trying to untangle what he'd said.

"Is Andrea pregnant?" She blurted out the worst fear first.

"What? Oh, hell, no."

"Are you in trouble with the police?" Summer heard the waterbed gurgle as he shook his head.

"Well, what? Tell me!" She was frightened now, and frustrated. "I can't help you if I don't know what it is."

Again the gurgle.

"Tulsa!"

The telephone cut into her cry, saving him. Tully rolled, reaching for it.

"Hello?" He listened, then sat up abruptly. "Just a second." Tully pressed the mouthpiece against his chest.

"Get out," he said sharply. The order piqued Summer.

He didn't have to be so mean. But his tone told her it was no time to pick a fight. She huffed up the stairs.

Tully watched her go, waiting until she had reached the top and slammed the door. Then he returned the receiver carefully to his mouth.

"Yeah. Hi, A.J."

• ELEVEN •

A.J. WAS LEANING against the telephone table, the sharp edge digging into his thigh. There was a chair, but he didn't sit. This was going to be a short call.

He cleared his throat to deepen his voice.

"Right. Uh. I'm calling about my weights," he said.

"They're still here," Tully said.

"Well, I'm kinda starting to get back into it . . . you know, lifting and . . ." A.J. took a breath. "I want them back."

There was a moment's heavy silence. A.J. could feel the stillness of his own house around him. Decco and June had gone to a movie. He couldn't have done this with anybody at home.

"Okay," Tully said at last. "Whatever you want. You can come get them anytime."

Now it was A.J.'s turn to choke. He had no way of getting the set back to his house. Tully was supposed to offer to bring them by. But he didn't, and A.J. couldn't ask. He had to give Tully more time to suggest it.

"Right," A.J. said, wrapping the telephone cord around his arm. "Too bad about the game tonight."

"Yeah. It always burns to lose a close one. Good thing we had Weitzammer and Millyard, or it wouldn't have been as close as it was."

"Right. Good thing." A.J. grappled. The cord was leaving little white marks on his bare arm. "Mendel had some sharp plays, too."

"You should have seen him in the third," Tully said.

A.J. had seen nothing but the locker room in the third period.

"Mendel's having a good year," A.J. said.

"Zarich, too," Tully said.

"And Kafke."

"And Lavalle."

"Lavalle's a jerk," A.J. blurted, the heat gushing from his stomach up to his chest.

There was a startled silence, then, "He can skate all right."

"You know what I mean. I've seen him in action. He's a first-class, manipulating jerk." The boy's heart was thudding wildly now, but he couldn't stop. All the things he'd been thinking this past week were cresting to the surface. "It's not your fault, Tul," A.J. continued, his voice hushed. "Lavalle can twist things around so you don't know what to think—I've seen him. But . . . but . . . don't let one mistake screw up your whole life."

"A.J. . . ." Tully started.

"You can get counseling, Tul. You're seventeen. They

wouldn't tell your parents or anything. Just cut him loose and you can get better. I know you can."

"Look, I know what you're getting at," Tully said shortly. "But don't sweat it, okay? You don't know what you're talking about."

"Lavalle is bad news!" A.J. insisted.

"He isn't my first lover."

A.J. stood, his pulse striking his temples like a drum, a bass drum, big and loud and empty.

"What?" he whispered. This was Chicco's all over again, only worse. This time there was no protective layer of doubt.

"You're sick," A.J. said.

Tully ignited. "What the hell century do you live in? We're talking about a lifestyle, not a disease."

"You're nuts," A.J. said. "You're out of your freaking head."

"You wanna talk about crazy? Going psycho on the ice, beating the crap out of some guy because it makes you feel like a bigshot—*that's* crazy."

There was no sound at the other end. Tully pushed ahead, steaming, only a trace of tremor in his voice.

"Anybody needs counseling, it's you, A.J. I'm not hurting anybody. You're the freaking menace. The cement heads at Riverview might think you're something, but Christ, you're embarrassing the whole—"

A.J. took the receiver away from his ear and replaced it in the cradle. Then he sat down in the waiting chair, carefully gripping the edge of the table.

Tully was lying, A.J. told himself. He just did it to cut me. What mattered to Landau, to everybody, was results, right? They weren't kids anymore. They all skated out expecting to get hit. That's how the league worked. And anyone who said different was a liar, or worse.

That night he dreamed of the game against the Terriers. He dreamed it so vividly that he could hear the hoarse, wrung-out voice of the crowd and feel the anxiety coiling around him like a boa constrictor. A.J. was in his own zone —the whole game seemed to be in his zone—and he scuffled and dug his way through the mess of jerseys. Everywhere he turned someone was blocking him. The puck skittered dangerously around the net, but the players were like a web. He couldn't see clearly or push them aside, and he was ready to scream in frustration when Bruce Fleury took the puck at the blue line. It was like a photograph, a perfect frame: Fleury and the puck and his own path of open ice.

A.J. felt the check, and for a brief second it was so solid, so satisfying. But Fleury buckled. He went down and he stayed down.

He's hurt—I've got to get him up, A.J. thought. He lurched forward and tried to lift the boy, but to his horror, Bruce began to fall apart. An arm hit the ice, then a leg, then another. A.J. clutched for the pieces, tried desperately to gather them all into his arms, but they kept falling. Then, at the edge of his vision, he saw the other players skating towards him and the panic slit up his torso like a knife. They couldn't see this!

"Get back!" he screamed. "I've got him—I'll carry him!"

He awoke on clammy sheets, his jaw so tight his teeth hurt. The cry was still locked in his mouth, tasting of iron. A.J. rolled slowly onto his side and laid his face in the cradle of his arm. He would carry Bruce Fleury. He would carry him for a long time.

November was a gray month. The snow fell and melted, then froze in the night, only to fall again the next day. Driving was treacherous and trucks sanded almost every day, until the entire city was the color and texture of gravel.

A.J. could feel the grit under his feet when he walked. Sometimes he could feel it even when he was inside, on the smooth, polished floor of Riverview High, or the thin, tired carpet in his house. Even worse was when the wind blew the sand into his clothes. The crawly, itchy, gritty feeling was maddening.

Paul Treejack and the others came by the house often, draping themselves like orangutans in the doorway while A.J. put on his sneakers. Somebody usually had a car, and they spent Saturday nights hanging around in parking lots and restaurants, trying to pick up girls.

They didn't usually do too well. For all his blustery arrogance with the guys, Paul Treejack turned to cardboard when confronted with the opposite sex. And Doerkson had the power to repel girls on contact.

"Hey!" he would call, approaching a prospective clutch of fifteen-year-old females. "Hey, didn't I see you in the August issue of *Stag*?"

The night would disintegrate after that.

What Doerkson said in public, though, was nothing compared to what Treejack said in private. When there were just three or four of them, cruising around or playing cards in somebody's basement, Treejack could hypnotize

them with tales of what he'd done, of what he was going
to do.

A.J. was no stranger to this stuff. Hockey locker rooms
were renowned for it. But Treejack wasn't just storytelling,
he was challenging.

A.J. would sweat, listening to the round robin of boast-
ing. Nobody ever said, "Okay, A.J., your turn," but he
knew. The gaps in the conversation taunted him.

So when the pressure was on and A.J. could feel the
quiet air pressed into a wedge on him, he delivered. He ran
out of the truth quickly. After that, he stretched and
shaped it. After that, he lied. Mostly about Jacquie, his old
girlfriend.

When he listened to himself, he became faintly sick.
Jacquie had been nice to him; he remembered how she
hugged. But she had moved away and she was safe.

"What about Summer Brown?" Doerkson asked once,
his eyes gleaming. "Jeez, she's a nice piece. Snotty, though;
wouldn't sit next to me on the van to Swift Current."

"Who would?" someone chortled in the background.
"Doerkson, you smell like a wet dog."

"Aw, come on," Doerkson said, grinning slyly at A.J.
"Don't tell me you can't score, Bad Boy. She's stuck on
you . . ." He trailed off expectantly. The whole room
seemed to pause, listening.

What can I say? A.J. wondered wildly. There was nothing to tell. He couldn't have even if there was. Summer
was private. Very private.

But they were waiting, all of them. Doerkson's ghastly
ghost-blue eyes were drilling into him. A.J. knew he was
pinned.

And so he smiled, forced his mouth into a slow, sly grin that felt like it was cracking his face.

Doerkson hooted and slapped his thigh. The room began to chatter again. Somebody cuffed A.J. on the shoulder. "Ooh, aren't you bad, boy!"

A.J. leaned back in his chair, the stupid grin still frozen in place. *I hate you, Doerkson*, was all he could think. *I hate your filthy guts.*

November waned and December dug in its heels. The air cooled and a light powdery snow covered the ugly frozen mush underneath. On the first Saturday night of the month, A.J. drove to Regina with Doerkson, Treejack and Rasmussen. They were looking for a bar.

The night crackled with potential. A.J. could feel it in the hum of the highway underneath Rasmussen's gas-guzzling Delta 88. The car was garbage compared to the Mustang, of course, but it was powerful, in a raw, brainless way, and the roar of the big V-8 was like music to A.J.

He was still flying high from the night before. The Cyclones had chalked up their third straight win, and against the second-ranked team in the league, too. A.J. had played his regular game, pushing, moving, agitating, but he'd had two assists—one while the team was short-handed.

How's that for a freaking menace? he wanted to shout. *Yeah, I really embarrassed the team. Not bad for a cement head, huh?*

The other cement heads were bouncing around the car like Doberman pinschers straining at their chains.

Rowdy, A.J. thought, grinning. Doerkson was almost

comical tonight, and A.J. found himself laughing occasion-
ally at the boy's sick jokes.

So he's a jerk, A.J. shrugged to himself. At least he's a
normal jerk. A.J. looked out at the dark prairie and passing
power poles that flickered in the strong light of the Delta's
high beams. He had two assists behind him and these safe
friends mortared like bricks around him. Bad Boy. It was
the best thing that could have happened. His shoulders felt
six feet wide in his denim and sheepskin jacket.

They picked a sagging cardboard box of a bar called
The Ranchman, because Rasmussen had heard that the
bouncers never asked for I.D. There were pool tables and
dart boards, chubby barmaids and truckers, all glazed by a
blanket of yellow light. A.J. counted fifteen black cigarette
burns in the tabletop before the glasses started coming.

"To a godawful Sunday morning and a helluva Saturday night!" Doerkson cried, struggling to be heard over
the blaring cowboy music. He raised his glass, slopping
draft.

This was a different kind of drinking, A.J. discovered.
This was nothing like wedding receptions—where you
danced—or house parties—where you played cards and
found people to talk to. This was line 'em up, belt 'em
back, and don't be the one with beer in your glass when
the waitress comes by again.

By ten o'clock his cheeks and mouth felt shot full of
novocaine. He tried to keep up with the conversation, but
he caught himself drifting, staring at the shiny rim of a
glass or a button on Treejack's shirt, and listening intently
to the songs that slithered out of the sound system.

He hated country and western, but tonight the music
seemed to seep into his skin. They were such simple songs,

raw with loneliness. Somebody was always hurting somebody else, or loving the wrong person, or loving the right person too late.

Why don't they just change things? A.J. wondered, turning his glass slowly in its own wet ring. Why don't they just find somebody new and start over? But he could hear why, he could hear it in every haunting note. Futility.

"Hey," Rasmussen said, jogging A.J.'s arm. "Aren't you a ball of fire tonight. You dead or what?"

A.J. looked up and tried to smile, but he wasn't sure if he succeeded. His face was too frozen.

"Treejack and I are going to shoot a game," Rasmussen said, starting to walk towards the pool tables. He looked at Doerkson. "Keep him breathing, hey?" Rasmussen said, jerking his head towards A.J.

Whatever tolerance A.J. had felt towards Doerkson earlier evaporated quickly. The gangly boy was in a talkative stage of drinking—eager, bold, stupid. He was sober enough to form sentences, but drunk enough not to care what he said.

"I cannot believe you," Doerkson said, his voice heavy with conspiracy. "I cannot believe you're so freakin' lucky. I mean she is just hot—so *hot.*" He stopped and giggled. "Summer—hot? Get it? Get it?"

A.J. stared, a statue. Doerkson pressed on blithely.

"You really gotta have something—know what I mean? She's just a kid, right? I seen her on the van and I think— whoa, that's a piece. But she's just a kid. Fourteen? Fifteen? And you're buddies with her brother, too. Christ!" Doerkson banged the table, laughing. "Her brother!"

From somewhere inside a pit, A.J. watched. All week

he'd felt sick about the unspoken lie they'd wrung out of him, but now he couldn't move a muscle to set it right.

"Tell me," Doerkson said, leaning so close that his gamey scent stung A.J.'s nose. "Is she as good as she looks? You know, clothes hide so much. And they can fake it, too. But when I saw her ass I thought, yeah, that's the real—"

A.J. stood up abruptly, his chair scraping. "I'll be back," he mumbled. He turned and headed for the men's room, banging his thigh on a table but not stopping, not even for a moment, to register the pain.

There were three sinks and six stalls, and a line of urinals against one green-tiled wall. It was a fair-sized room, but grimy. The floor was suspiciously damp. No one else was there, but A.J. was too self-conscious to use a urinal. He went into a stall and closed the door.

He caught himself swaying as he stood there. Time seemed to be a ribbon, full of loops and knots. How much had passed? One minute? Ten? He didn't know and it didn't matter. He was just zipping up his fly when he heard the dripping faucet.

A.J. put his hand on the gray cubicle wall, listening. A sink was plugged and had filled with water. The steady *drip, drip* distorted in the hollow room. The echo was metallic. The longer he listened, the louder it got, and the more it sounded like a hammer hitting a tin roof, or the beating of his own metal heart.

It came on him suddenly. It came on him so fast he almost betrayed himself with a sound. One moment he was just listening and the next he was suffocating, his eyes scalding and his throat in a tourniquet.

It frightened him. For the first time all night he knew

exactly what he was feeling and who he was feeling it about, and it scared him to death.

Oh, for Christ's sake, he swore at himself, brushing at his eyes with the heel of his palm. Oh, just *don't*. But alone in the cubicle, with no one to judge him, he couldn't fight the rush of memory, and sensation, and loss.

Then the men's room door opened, and a gust of bar-room noise blew in.

"A.J.?" Treejack called softly.

The boy closed his burning eyes. Go away, he pleaded.

Treejack's sneakers squeaked over the wet floor. Only one stall was closed, only one had feet under it. Treejack grabbed the top of A.J.'s door and rattled it loudly.

"Hey! Are you okay in there?"

Leave me alone, A.J. begged. Get the hell away from me. For a moment there was only Treejack's rapid breath, and the dripping tap.

Treejack swore out loud, certain that A.J. had passed out. He stepped back and kicked violently at the door. The feeble lock gave, and the door blasted into the cubicle.

Backed up against the side wall, A.J. felt the slam of air. Then Treejack had him by the shoulders.

"You nimrod," Treejack muttered, pushing A.J. out of the cubicle. "What were you doing? We left twenty minutes ago."

It was too much, too close. A.J. turned hard, his elbow up. Treejack caught it across the shoulder and chest, and went staggering back. He was no hockey player; he didn't know how to duck a check.

Treejack stared, furious, bewildered. "What the . . . ?"

"Don't touch me," A.J. said, his big arms still up, ready. "Don't you ever touch me."

Treejack opened his mouth, then shut it. He was no match for A.J. Brandiosa, drunk or sober. He dropped his angry glare and pushed past A.J. roughly.

"Save it for the ice, Bad Boy," he muttered.

· TWELVE ·

A.J. WAS TRYING *not* to save it for the ice. Every practice, every game, he skated out thinking, Be *smart,* A.J. Move the puck. Get your head up. But it was so hard.

The problem was that they were winning. In the last six games, the Cyclones had won four, tied one, and lost one. Habits became ceremonies, quirks became intense rituals. If you'd worn a certain T-shirt the night the streak began, you wore it every time you played—unwashed. If you'd skated on dull blades, they stayed dull.

A.J. knew his own talisman. He wished it were something as simple as a T-shirt. He would tape his stick as methodically, as precisely as ever, promising that *this* game he would play smart and straight and show those jerks who was a goon and who wasn't.

But even as he made the vow he would feel a clutch of panic in his chest. What if he did let up, and they lost? What if this game, they really needed an enforcer?

Landau had called him that—enforcer. It had been two

games ago, the night they'd come up against the second-ranked Tri-Stars. In his pregame briefing, Landau had said, ". . . and Grummett and Rudachuk, I want you all over this Daniels. Keep him buried. If he gets out in front, he's deadly. And enforcer"—Landau had looked directly at A.J.—"enforce. They're running a real goon squad this year. Don't wait—push back *first."* The coach had closed up his notes. "We could be in for a wild ride tonight."

It had been that—a game of high sticks and hair-trigger tempers. The second period took forever to play. It was studded with clashes.

It wasn't just me, A.J. thought. But it felt like it was just me.

The home crowd was coming to know him. After two periods of traded goals—and elbows and profanities—the crowd was roaring every time A.J. made a check. Just into the third period, Weitzammer got himself into a blistering altercation. When A.J. chucked his gloves to get Weitzammer out of it, the noise in the arena almost lifted him out of his skates.

A.J. took his five-minute penalty without complaint. He accepted the tied game without regret. He carried the sound home with him and took it to bed, thinking, They love this. No matter what Lloyl says in the paper, or all the fuss about violence and sports, they love this.

It frightened him how it made his heart pound. He struggled to squeeze it into perspective; he struggled for control. But the crowd and their noise and the name—his name—kept him thinking until he could fall asleep. It kept him safe.

And A.J. knew he wasn't safe. Ever since the night of the bar and the bathroom in Regina, he'd had to be on

guard. If he didn't focus—on the game or something specific—he knew what he would think about. He knew how
he would feel. It could creep up on him anytime: doing lab
experiments at school; showering after practice; but especially when he was lying naked under the covers, waiting
for sleep.

He tried to shame himself. This is sick, A.J. It's crazy.
Just *stop,* for Christ's sake, he ordered desperately. But the
feeling would not stop. It crept up and overwhelmed him
with its heavy, hypnotic heat.

He would not give in. Even when his mouth was swimming and the rest of him was bursting, he rolled over onto
his stomach, his hands clenched into fists under the pillow.
He was so lonely he wanted to die.

The last week before Christmas vacation was cold and
frantic. Midterm exams seemed to come on more abruptly
than any other year, and A.J. found himself scrambling to
absorb the information that he'd scrawled in his notebooks.
He couldn't remember taking it down. Even biology, one
of his best subjects, was a blur.

To make matters worse, the temperature dropped to a
bone-chilling minus twenty-five, and stayed there. It was
an ordeal just walking to school. Last year he hadn't had to
face any of this. The Mustang had just appeared at his
door, sometimes late but always warm. Now the air
seemed to freeze his nostrils shut, and the snow was as
brittle as Styrofoam under his sneakers. Midway through
his first class every morning, his ears and toes sang with
pain.

It was a bitter Wednesday morning when Treejack
showed up at his locker. A.J. had just arrived, lightheaded

from the sudden shock of warm air, still blinking the condensation out of his eyes. He could barely see the numbers on his combination lock.

"Hi," Treejack said.

"Hi," A.J. said, but he kept concentrating on his locker. He had been avoiding Treejack lately, or maybe they had been avoiding each other since their skirmish in the men's room of The Ranchman.

"I'm having this party," Treejack said. "Sort of a midterm, Christmas bash. Saturday night. You want to be there?"

A.J. felt a small gush of relief and forced an apologetic smile up on his face. "Sorry—can't. We've got a game." It wasn't a lie. The Cyclones were pairing off against the first-ranked Broncos. A.J. had been tied up in knots about it for days.

"Yeah, but it's an early game, right?" There was just the hint of a twist to Treejack's smile. "You'll be out of the arena by nine. Lots of time. Get loaded and celebrate. Bring a girl. Bring Summer Brown."

A.J. started, he knew he did. And Treejack knew it, too, even though A.J. was staring intently into his locker, pretending to shuffle through his books. But the boy managed to shrug his big shoulders. "Kinda short notice," he said.

"Oh, come on." Treejack cuffed him, a deliberate taunt. "She's just so *wild* for you, right? She couldn't say no to A.J. Brandiosa, defense superstar. Not after she's been saying yes again and again and again . . ."

A.J. looked up sharply, the skin on his face stretched taut and white.

"And you *like* Summer Brown, don't you, Bad Boy?"

Treejack said softly, eyes glittering. "You do *like* girls . . ."

A.J. caught him so fast Treejack sucked in his breath. One arm, one strong arm, was all it took to pin him hard against the lockers.

"What the fuck are you saying?"

Treejack's eyes were wide with fear, but he knew he had the upper hand. A.J. would not risk suspension by fighting in the hall. He pretended hurt astonishment.

"Hey, back off! I'm just doing you a favor. You know, being nice?"

Treejack's voice carried. A.J. became aware of where he was again, and that people were watching him. Self-consciously he let Treejack go.

"What kind of a favor?" he said, unable to keep from clipping the words.

Treejack took his time straightening his clothes. "The spare room," he said finally. "In my basement. I'll save it for you and Summer. Nobody'll bother you. You two can have your own private party." Now he did smirk. "That is, if you want it."

He didn't wait for an answer, but started walking away slowly. "I'll tell everybody you two are coming. We'll watch for you. And, hey . . . loosen up, Bad Boy."

A.J. could not loosen up. He could hardly breathe. He watched Treejack's back disappear into the current of kids. There were only three possible reasons for what had just occurred.

Treejack was punishing him for his outburst in the bar. He was punishing him, and this innuendo was the lowest, cruelest shot he could think of. Or else the sky had fallen and Treejack had found out about A.J.'s old friend, Tulsa Brown.

Or else, A.J. thought, a slow chill crawling over his scalp, he was somehow wearing his nightmare on his face and the whole world, including Treejack, could see it.

"I can't believe you!" Summer said, charging ahead, not looking at him. "You've got more guts than brains."

A.J. had caught up with her on the way home from school, before she got to her bus stop. His legs were longer than hers, and she had the handicap of high-heeled boots, but still he had to struggle to keep up.

"Look, I said I was sorry," he mumbled into the collar of his jacket.

"Funny how you're sorry now, not a month ago."

He knew she was referring to the game in Swift Current where he hadn't so much as waved.

"You said come and I came," Summer continued. "I had to drive down on a bus full of sick perverts, because my ignoramus brother is too stuck up to let me ride with him and his friends. But I came."

For a moment the only sound was the snow squeaking under their feet. "Do you realize I hate that stupid game?" she said, a quiver of despair in her voice. "I spent two hours in that freezing arena watching something I literally despise . . ."

All so that I could see you. She didn't have to say it. A.J.'s chest felt like a cavern under his jacket. He'd hardly thought about Summer or the game in Swift Current. But now, so close, absorbing her the way he used to, the realization struck him full in the face: the day was a wound to her.

You stupid, stupid ass, he cursed. He didn't want to take her to Treejack's party. He didn't want to take her anywhere near that grimy bunch.

But panic knee-jerked him back to reality. He didn't have a choice. All he could see was Treejack's face, his intent, merciless eyes. You *like* Summer Brown, don't you, Bad Boy? You do *like* girls . . .

"I had a bad game," A.J. said, as if that would explain everything.

Summer sighed, a short blast of irritation. "The *game* again! Don't you guys have anything else in your lives? Tully snaps my head off every time I talk to him. What is it? A bad game. You invite me out to see you, then treat me like dirt. What's the problem? A bad game."

Her legs had caught up to her anger; she was hurrying again. "Well, I'm sick to death of the *game*, A.J. God, how can you let it manipulate your whole life?"

They had arrived at the bus stop, and went inside the Plexiglas shelter to wait, settling against opposite walls. It was warmer here without the wind, and quieter. Summer leaned on her shoulder and stared out the doorway. A.J. leaned on his back and stared at Summer.

Her tilted chin and wind-wild hair cut a crisp silhouette against the clear plastic. She held herself straight with anger and indignation, but sideways, she seemed slight. A knot swelled and hardened in A.J.'s throat.

"You just think I'm always there," Summer said suddenly, her gaze still pinned on the street. "You don't call, you never come by. When you pop up you expect me to drop at your feet."

A.J. didn't move.

"And I'm not Godzilla," she continued. "You're talking

about Saturday night. Did it ever occur to you that I might already have a date?"

Of course it hadn't. He hadn't thought about any of it, just rushed out blindly after her in the schoolyard, a desperate, unthinking interception.

"I'm not good at this," A.J. said, his frozen breath catching on his sheepskin collar. "I . . . I don't go out with a lot of girls. Maybe I don't always think straight or I don't know how to do things right, and I come off sounding like a jerk." The knot in his throat was the size of a golf ball. "I like you," he said finally. "It's not always easy to like you, but I do. I don't know what else you want me to say."

Summer didn't reply; her expression hadn't changed. A.J. dug his hands deep into his pockets thinking, to hell with Treejack. I can't do this. He wanted to push himself off the wall and say, "Well, maybe some other time, okay?" and vanish.

There was a sound in the distance and they both looked up to see the Number 18 cresting a curve a few blocks away.

"My bus is coming," Summer said. She took a deep breath. "What time Saturday night?"

A.J. stepped forward, hardly daring to believe. "Nine o'clock. Could . . . could you meet me at the arena, by the dressing room? We'll go from there."

"I won't watch you play," Summer said. They could hear the big diesel engine now as the bus surged closer.

"No," A.J. agreed, following her out onto the sidewalk. "I don't have a car. We'll have to walk, if that's all right," he finished apologetically.

Summer smiled a crooked little smile. It was the first

comfortable moment since they'd left Riverview High, and the Number 18 pulled up, ending it.

Summer turned. "I'd ask Tully to drive us—"

"No, don't." A.J. cut her off. "Don't ask him, don't tell him. Please?"

"Well, he probably wouldn't anyway. He's been in such a snit lately," she said, starting up the bus's steps. "I don't know what his problem is."

I do, and I wish I didn't, A.J. thought. "See you Saturday," he called, stepping back. Summer looked over her shoulder but the doors slapped shut and the dinosaur rumbled away, blasting the boy with noise and wind and diesel fumes. He watched the square back end until it was gone.

I'll make it up to her. It's going to be all right, he told himself over and over as he started the long walk home, his feet striking the snow as mechanically as clockwork.

· THIRTEEN ·

A.J. WAS WRONG. Sex was never a problem for Tully. Sex was a song that started in his head; he could hear it a long time before he was touched. It had rhythm and tone and heat. It started in his head but it sang in his body, and like all good songs, he could lose himself in it. Sometimes it was loud and fast, hard rock driven by raw guitar. Sometimes it was soft and slow, the very last number they played at the prom. Sometimes it was even air-guitar, a dance you danced alone, just for joy.

The problem was when the music stopped. Tully knew that moment. At a school dance or a wedding, there was sometimes a gap between the ending of one song and the beginning of another. You looked around, feeling stupid and shy, painfully aware you were standing with a stranger.

Downstairs at Derek's house, in the rich, paneled rec room, the music had stopped. Tully trailed his fingers along the wall; he liked the unfinished texture of real wood. These last few weeks he had come to know this room so well—its walls and tables and pictures and bed. Funny how you could come to know a room, and not the person who inhabited it. He felt very, very alone.

"What time is it?" Derek said.

"I don't know." Tully didn't move.

"Well, look, then. You're the one with the watch."

"It's dark. I couldn't read it even if I could find it."

Derek let out a short exasperated breath. Tully heard the frustration and was glad. He'd been trying to short-circuit Derek's cool lately, tear holes in the web he'd felt closing around him. At first it had been a game, but he didn't want to play anymore. Ownership wasn't friendship.

Soon he got up. The rustle of clothing seemed loud in the silence.

"I'm going home," Tully said.

"Why? It's still early."

"I want to do some lifting," Tully said, zipping up his jeans.

Derek sat up.

"Oh, right. I forgot. His weights are *still* at your place. It'd be a real problem to drop them off to him. He lives on the other side of the world."

Tully paused, his muscles tensing. He had laid down very few rules with Derek, even fewer here, in this room. But since the night at Chicco's, one rule was absolute. Don't talk about A.J. Don't ask about him. Don't bad-mouth him.

Tully continued moving, pulling his shirt cautiously over his head, slipping into his runners.

"Just can't say good-bye, can you, Tulsa?" Derek said softly. "What are you hoping for? Take it from me, partydoll. Don't break your heart on a straight. Or maybe I'm wrong." He paused. "You just never know, right? Maybe there's something the world doesn't know about the Big Bad Defense. Like maybe he's just real, real care—"

Derek slammed against the headboard. He was frozen, by surprise and pain. His back and neck and shoulders were pinned helplessly. Tully's fists were full of dark hair.

"Don't," Tully said, the word a blast of winter in Derek's eyes. "Don't even think about it. You smear him and you won't have a face left to show in public. I promise you." Slam. "It's a small town, *partydoll,* a small fucking town."

Tully pushed away, hard. He turned on his heel and strode out of the room, swiping his jacket from the chair as he passed. Up the stairs, out the door, to his car. When he tried to put the key into the ignition, he missed. He tried once more and it was worse. He looked down at the key, but it was shaking so badly he closed his hand around it. The ridges dug into his palm. Tully stared at the steering wheel through water, then he hammered it with the side of his fist. And again. And again.

It was after six o'clock when he pulled up to his house. His father was shoveling snow off the walk, bent over as he dug, his beard frosted white. He looked so old. It was as though twenty years had passed since that morning, and Tully was coming home to a place that wasn't the same.

Tully got out of the car and put on his mitts. He found the old shovel on the back porch. The family called it the bad shovel because the handle was cracked and came out of the socket sometimes. But if you lifted just right and tilted

the snow off instead of tossing it, the shovel stayed together. Tully dug into the shadowed drifts that covered the
long path on the side of the house.

The snow was wet and heavy. He had to dig the wide
blade in and lift, not scoop. In a few minutes his muscles
were blazing, and he was gulping the cold air like water.

Still, he liked it, the simpleness of it, the familiarity.
And when he glanced behind him and saw the clean, clear
trail he had cut, it was a relief somehow. Tully tore into
the drifts ahead.

He was working so intently that the end of the walk
came as a surprise. He struck grass and dirt so hard he
almost dislocated his shoulder. Tully swore out loud and
straightened up, and then he saw that his father was watching him.

"I thought it was your turn to cook tonight, not
shovel," Tully said, wiping the sleeve of his jacket across
his damp forehead. He always felt awkward when his dad
caught him cursing.

Mr. Brown was leaning on his shovel. "I don't know. I
just felt like it." He nodded towards the fresh path. "You
did a good job. Thanks." Then he touched Tully's cheek
with his mitt. "You know what Grandma would say your
reward is?"

Tully grinned ruefully. "Apple cheeks."

"Since I'm the one cooking, supper can wait. You want
to go for a ride, get something warm to drink?" Mr.
Brown asked, setting his shovel against the side of the
house.

Tully hesitated. He knew he was treading water right
now, too tired to swim, too frightened to sink. To be alone

with someone who loved him, someone who would listen to him, was a dangerous thing.

But his father looked so hopeful. For months they had only been passing each other in the doorway. "Sure," Tully said, and he leaned his shovel next to the other.

They met on the driver's side of the Mustang, both expecting the wheel. There was an awkward pause, and then Tully relinquished the keys. He forgot sometimes whose car it really was.

Mr. Brown started the engine and eased it into gear. Tully couldn't believe how gently his father shifted, how lightly he stepped on the brake and the gas. The boy felt a twinge remembering how he had just gunned the old car up and down Moose Jaw's main strip, trying to burn away the memory of the afternoon.

"You know, the Mustangs were originally advertised as the ideal ladies' car," Mr. Brown said suddenly.

"You're kidding," Tully said. In his own eyes—and everyone else's—it was the consummate muscle car, the one that looked fast in the parking lot.

"Really. I've got the magazine ad to prove it. And you know why they sold it as a ladies' car?"

"Why?"

"You have to lock the door with the ignition key." His father looked at him and winked. "So you can't lock the keys in the car." Tully burst into surprised laughter. "And if you tell your mother I said that, I'll kill you!"

Tully loved it. He sat grinning for a long time.

They drove around the little city, the purpose of the ride forgotten. The streetlights had come on and passed over the Mustang's hood with calming regularity. The tension didn't leave Tully, but it loosened its grip on him.

Sitting in the passenger seat, he felt like a kid again, any kid, out for a ride with his dad.

How long had it been, he wondered, since it had been so easy to be with someone? Since autumn, he thought with a pang. Since A.J.

Then his father said, "So, what's new?" and Tully took a deep breath.

"Dad . . . I want to quit the team."

The boy could feel the shock from across the car. For a moment there was no sound.

"Why?" Mr. Brown said quietly.

"Because it isn't fun anymore," Tully said, wringing the leather mitts on his lap. "Because everybody takes it so seriously, you know? If you lose you feel like garbage, and if you win you get strung out wondering how you're going to keep winning. It isn't just a bunch of guys going out to play the best they can. Everybody's so psyched out that you start blaming each other and maybe you even hate each other . . ." He trailed off, too close to the nerve.

"Well, what did you think it was going to be like when you tried out for the team?" his father asked.

Tully was stumped. During the whirlwind of tryouts, he hadn't thought of anything except playing the best he could and impressing Landau. And getting picked was such a rush. That had carried him for a long time. But somehow not long enough.

Another high dive, Tully thought. Another wild leap with his eyes closed and the pool bottom coming up too fast. And he knew without thinking that he picked teams the way he chose lovers, the way he found a party, or lost a friend.

"Look," Mr. Brown said, cutting into his thoughts,

"this is your decision. But you've made a commitment to this team. Why don't you wait until after the Christmas break? It might be different after everyone's had a rest."

Tully nodded. But as they rounded the last corner for home, he knew that some things would not wait until after Christmas; some things were finished now. He hoped he wasn't too late.

· FOURTEEN ·

A.J. WOKE WITH a painful start Saturday morning. He sat up, expecting to rush somewhere, or cram for something. For a few moments he waited, blinking in the darkness, before he realized that exams were over.

He looked at the clock and grimaced: 5:15 A.M. The alarm hadn't even been set. He thought about going back to sleep, but he couldn't. An exam-awakening was like an ice-water treatment.

A hot shower helped. In the second-floor bathroom he tried to scrub the week away—the frenzy of studying, the anxiety of asking Summer out. The soap had an herbal smell—unfamiliar but nice—and afterwards he just stood under the water, absorbing the heat and sensation. A shower was a little miracle, A.J. thought. It could make you feel human again.

He didn't dress to go downstairs, just pulled on a bathrobe. He couldn't bear to put jeans, underwear and a shirt on his talc-smooth body. He felt too good, too free.

He smelled the coffee on the landing, the smell of some-one awake and at home, and he was surprised by how glad he was. He was hungry for company. His father worked shifts, and A.J. could never keep track of which Saturdays he had off.

Just be nice, A.J. told himself. Don't even bring up the subject of her. Be nice and just talk to him, and don't get worked up into a sweat. Maybe it'll be a nice day. It had been so long since he'd felt hopeful. The first lights of dawn lit up his wet hair as he walked into the kitchen.

He stopped cold. June was sitting at the kitchen table wearing one of his father's old bathrobes. She looked plain and girlish without makeup, and she had her feet up on another chair. The robe opened above her knees, and the shock of bare skin seemed miles long.

Her eyes widened. She obviously hadn't been expecting him at this hour on a Saturday. A.J. turned abruptly to the counter.

She slept here, he thought, his fingertips pressed on the countertop, bracing him. She spent the night with my father.

A wave of disgust whipped through him. It seemed incomprehensible. His dad was forty-three years old, for Christ's sake. *His* dad. This was vile. They were both vile.

His first impulse was to bolt from the room. Then he realized that his robe only came to midthigh. He was horribly vulnerable.

But shock was kindling into anger. This is my house, not hers, A.J. thought. Anybody should feel unwanted, it's her. She already felt too bloody at home as it was. He had to show her, put her in her place. A.J. groped for the bag of muffins, conscious only of the edge of his nightrobe rubbing his skin four inches above his knee.

June had regained her poise. "Good morning," she said.

A.J. split a fresh carrot muffin and began to butter it. The butter was cold and tore the soft insides apart.

"Where's my dad?"

"At work. You're up early for a day you don't have to go to school." She sounded so cool, so sure of herself.

"How old are you?" he asked suddenly.

There was a pause. "I don't think that's any of your business."

A.J. twisted halfway around to meet her eyes, keeping the front of his robe towards the cupboards. "Yeah, I think it *is* my business," he said evenly. "You're sitting in my house."

"This is your father's house," she said, "and I am his guest, Allan James."

The boy's temperature sparked and flared. He hated his full name; he never told it to people. That she should know it—and use it—made him feel even more naked.

"The name's A.J.," he said hotly.

"And I'm June Fehr," she said. "How do you do."

A.J. was aware that he was breathing too fast. What kind of woman was this? In all the time she had spent here, he had spoken to her directly maybe three times. A.J. allowed himself to absorb her cautiously with his eyes.

Her bare feet were flat on the floor now, knees drawn together, comfortable. How could she sit there, naked under his father's bathrobe, after a night of God knew what, and look so . . . *dignified*?

He turned his back on her and began to eat his muffin over the sink. The memory of her bare legs burned in his mind. He pressed himself against the cupboards to keep what was happening from happening.

"Why are you doing this?" he asked.

"Doing what?"

Screwing around with an old man, he wanted to say. "Going out with my dad," he said. "Leading him on."

June laughed, a clear, surprised sound as light as sea spray. "I know you're not going to believe this," she said, "but I like him."

"You're young enough to be his daughter," A.J. said thickly.

The kitchen fell into silence. A.J. exulted that he had hit the nerve, stung her. But when June started to speak, she sounded serious, not hurt.

"Did it ever occur to you that that's not your concern?" June said. "Did you ever think there was a part of your father that has nothing to do with you?"

A.J. straightened. I'm his freaking *kid,* he wanted to shout. It's got everything to do with me.

June stood up. He heard the rustle as she tightened the bathrobe belt.

"I like your dad a lot," she said. "I want to like you, too. But it's not necessary, A.J. Your dad doesn't need your permission to be happy."

And then she touched him. On her way out of the kitchen she reached up and patted his back, between his shoulder blades. It jarred him worse than if she'd screamed at him.

He stared out the kitchen window, angry and aroused and perplexed and just a little in awe of her.

•

"By the time I hit the blue line, I want you at the point," Mendel was saying.

"Right," Kafke said.

"Not before," Mendel said. "Don't get there and sit like a moron. *Coast* into it. Be sly, for Christ's sake. But when I get to the blue line, *be* there."

"Yeah, right," Kafke said irritably.

"And be ready," Mendel stressed. "Because as soon as I pass, I'm gonna snap. Give and go."

Give and go. It was one of the simplest passing maneuvers in the book, one of the first combinations you learned. But Mendel was explaining it as though Kafke were new to the planet.

"Don't jerk around," Mendel said. "Just take it and let go again. Nothing fancy. Got it?"

"I got it, I got it!" Kafke snapped. "For cryin' out loud, Mendel, I've been playing this game since I was *six.*"

He turned abruptly and moved away, disgusted.

"Just *be* there! You hear me?" Mendel called after him. There was no response. A.J. heard Mendel thunk his stick irritably on the spongy black floor.

They were good friends, Kafke and Mendel. They had played together, on and off, for a long time. This was going to be one of those games, A.J. thought.

The locker room was abnormally quiet, the silence magnified by the little bursts of conversation, short and intense. Tempers were strung like tripwires across the room.

The guys were usually so revved before a game, especially lately, with the wins stacking up like poker chips. Tonight was different. Tonight they were tuned into themselves, their own rituals, their own rhythms.

Even Landau was on edge. He had never been a jovial

coach, but after the first few games, he had treated them like adults, sort of. Maybe lesser adults. Now as he mingled among them, barking orders, goading them, A.J. felt an uncomfortable pull backwards to the beginning of the season.

"All right, *gentlemen*," Landau said. "I think you know what you're up against."

They did. The Cyclones had played the first-ranked Broncos early in the season, in exhibition. A.J. remembered the wild run of that game, sprinter's pace, and the stunning 10–1 loss that had left them feeling raw. The Broncos had serious talent. Three of their players had already been signed for Junior hockey, two of them in major cities.

"No B.S. and no backtalk. I don't care what kind of streak you think you're on." The lines looked cut into Landau's face. "Run your patterns and *hustle*, every single second you're on. Or they're going to make you look like a joke—and not a private one, either."

A.J. knew it was true. Scouts had the tendency to show up at Bronco games. The team brought out the best—and worst—in their opposition. They also merited newspaper space. Ted Lloyl had almost taken them up as his personal cause. Yeah, it's real tough to cheer for number one, A.J. thought acidly. But Lloyl applauded the Broncos' "clean style, aggressive but smart. These young men spend their time skating, not brawling. Considering their position in the league, that should tell you something about how the game should be played."

A.J. was already wound up for this contest. Knowing that Ted Lloyl was probably sitting out there, pen poised for vindication, made his palms swim and his mouth run dry. He would have sold his soul to have his two assists back, to have them happen tonight.

Instead, he concentrated. For real this time, A.J. vowed. No matter what happens, no matter what Landau wants, you're not going to play the bruiser tonight.

The Cyclones knew what to expect from the Broncos. They had read about them, analyzed them, dissected their style. But it didn't make a bit of difference. A.J. skated out into what felt like a windstorm. The forwards were nimble, quick-thinking. When they were in the Cyclone end, A.J. found himself scrambling to keep up to them, never mind ahead of them.

And that wasn't his only problem. He found himself running into a lot of elbows. The Broncos hit him at the slightest excuse. If they got him to the boards, they dug in hard. For this team, touted for its lack of violence, it was unnatural.

A.J.'s first reflex was to get mad, but he reined himself back by trying to think it through. Were they trying to provoke him into a penalty? Or were they—he felt a stab of déjà vu—just giving him the message that they wouldn't put up with bulldozing?

It could be either, A.J. thought. But something occurred to him as he settled onto the bench, his shift over. They had been slamming him, not guarding him. No one had seemed too concerned when he was close to the puck, not like they were with Weitzammer or Pilka or Lavalle.

They had bought it, A.J. realized, a shiver running over him. The Bad Boy image. It was all they expected of him. A.J. leaned forward, his eyes fastening onto the play, tuning it into focus.

Weitzammer was taking a beating. Every time he stepped onto the ice, the Broncos deliberately cranked up the pace. Even when he didn't have the puck, they rode him incessantly. His shifts became shorter and shorter, and he came off open-mouthed, gasping, too tired even to swear.

It soon dawned on A.J. why they were so afraid of Weitzammer. The Bronco hotshots were as dangerous as promised; they were play-makers, combo workers. But they had to be—they were working in front of a weak net.

He didn't get much of a chance to be sure; most of the first period was spent in the Cyclone end. But whenever the play crept over center ice, his eyes were riveted to the goalie.

He's moving too far out of the crease, A.J. thought. He's moving out too far and too soon. The few blocks the goalie made were shoddy. He had to scramble for saves Terry Frances could make in his sleep. If it came to a one-on-one with Weitzammer—or almost anybody—this goaltender would lose. But in the first period, it never came to that. The Cyclones trooped wearily into the dressing room, down 2–0.

Landau was walking three inches off the ground.

"I cannot believe this," he said, biting the words. "What the hell are you doing out there? Pilka—somebody tape your elbows down? They won't break off if you use them, you know." He swiveled around. "And Lavalle, I'd say you were stoned if I didn't know you were such a lazy S.O.B."

Landau stung, and stung again. They were sloppy, they

were disorganized. They were letting Weitzammer do all the work.

Despite it all, A.J. could not keep down the hope that kept bobbing in him like a cork. For Pete's sake, we're up against the first-place team, he thought. The last time we played the Broncos, we were down *four* nothing by now. So we're twice as good as we were.

And he was thinking about something else. A surprise. If the chance came up. The idea was so sweet that he grinned as he readied himself for the next period. He lifted his head to put on his helmet and caught Tully watching him from across the room, curious, intent. A.J. turned abruptly and headed for the door.

He had a good second period, now that his vision had sharpened. He consciously toned down his movements to textbook defense, doing what he had to to get by. He even had a few smooth plays—skillfully creating an opening for Kafke, who was trapped behind the net—that set his insides humming.

You're doing okay, A.J. told himself. Lloyl can't pick you apart tonight. You'll be all right—even if your chance doesn't come up.

But it did.

At the eight-minute mark, the puck was in the Cyclone end, as usual. A Bronco forward had it at the end line, near the boards. Normally it would be A.J.'s job to guard him, but for some reason, Grummett was already there, and A.J. was at the point. Trapped, the forward turned and shot, hoping to deflect it off the boards to his defenseman, who was waiting at the blue line.

As soon as the forward released, A.J.'s stomach flipped.

Bad angle—too sharp. He lunged, and intercepted the puck just outside the point.

The Bronco defenseman hadn't moved. He didn't expect the *goon* to carry the puck. A.J. was supposed to pass.

Jackpot! A.J. bolted forward, praying somebody had anticipated this, praying somebody was there.

"Side!" Tully screamed. A.J. let the shot fly, just a breath in front of the blue line. The puck went winging across the ice, where Tully caught it in front of the center line.

A.J. was barreling down the ice. He had surprised the Bronco defenseman, captured himself a few precious seconds' head start, but he knew it couldn't last. Already he sensed the Bronco gaining, and his lungs were on fire.

Then, at the edge of his vision, he saw it—Tully winding up for the pass. It was like a slam of electricity. A.J. lurched forward without thinking, and the next thing he knew he was flying over the Bronco blue line, the puck on his stick.

Oh, shit, now what? his insides cried. He never got this far. He couldn't remember which was his best shot. He couldn't remember if he *had* a best shot. The goalie had moved out, anticipating. A.J. sucked in his breath and fired, not even sure which corner of the net he was aiming for.

The top right. The Cyclones screamed like idiots. They pounded him until his exhausted body almost collapsed. But moments later he was dancing on the ice, swimming in the second sweet flood of adrenaline.

All right! his heart sang. All goddamn right! When he finally skated for the bench, he was certain he could have skipped up the seats to the roof of the arena, in his skates.

Just in front of the gate, an arm caught him around the neck and he was jerked back into a headlock. He felt a glove cuff his helmet.

"Great play," Tully said. "Jesus! Great play."

He released A.J., pushing him forward so that the husky defenseman almost stumbled into the box. A.J. kept going, too startled to react. He dropped into his seat and fixed his eyes on the play, which had started again. His cheeks were burning.

You, too, A.J. thought. Great play, Tul. But he couldn't have said it out loud.

The goal energized a tired team. The Cyclones leapt into the second half of the period. But the Broncos were leaping, too. In the fading seconds, one of the Bronco "Super Three" nailed in an unassisted point. The Cyclones dragged themselves in for another session with Landau, again down by two.

A.J. sat with the others. He listened. He looked properly chastened.

But you can't take this away from me, he thought stubbornly. He knew it was a selfish attitude. His team was in real danger of losing. But it was his first goal of the year and a triumph—a goal against the top team in the league. And nobody was going to make it anything less.

Landau ran out of steam early, leaving them to brood. The gathering scattered, some into little groups, some alone. A.J. wandered down a corridor of lockers and sat by himself. Just for now, he thought. Just for a little while and then I'll be finished and ready for whatever's next.

And when he was soaking in it, the rush of it, the heat and the sound of them, not cheering but screaming—he felt something clunk down beside him on the bench. A.J. looked. It was a skate. Derek Lavalle's skate.

Lavalle was leaning forward on his knee, grinning. His helmet was off and his hair was bright with sweat. He seemed all pinpricks of light—teeth and hair and eyes.

"Good goal, Brandiosa," Lavalle said.

A.J. stood up. He was not at ease with this guy towering over him. "Thanks," he said flatly. Then he waited.

"It was wild," Lavalle said, still grinning. "The last thing they expected—hell, the last thing *we* expected. The two of you set that up or what?"

"No," A.J. said. "Just luck."

Lavalle shook his head, righting himself. There was almost a chuckle bubbling under his voice. "Well, it didn't look like luck. Goddamned good play," he said, turning to go.

A.J. stared at Lavalle's back in disbelief. Then he took a cautious deep breath.

Three lockers from the end of the corridor, Lavalle turned, as if he had forgotten something. "Oh, by the way. He's all yours."

A.J.'s nerves contracted in one quick, painful yank. "What?" he said.

The winger gazed back serenely. "You know. The golden boy. Hey, I know when I'm beat. I'm bowing out gracefully. He's all yours."

"I don't know what the hell you're talking about." The words clunked out as stiff, as unwieldy as bricks.

Lavalle's mouth twisted into a smirk. "Lying faggot," he said.

· FIFTEEN ·

"... Miserable snot-nosed punk!" Landau shouted in his face.

A.J. was flattened against the wall. His shoulder hurt. The side of his head hurt. Despite the protective pads, Landau's knuckles were digging into his collarbone, and that hurt, too.

The coach shoved against him once more, mostly in frustration, then pushed himself off. Released, A.J. staggered. He caught himself and looked up, right into Landau's laser eyes.

"You're not good enough, mister—*nobody's* good enough—to pull that schoolyard shit in here."

A.J.'s gaze darted. The entire team had clustered around, their faces blank with disbelief. Against a set of lockers he saw Lavalle, one arm still pinned by Millyard. A rust-red smudge trailed under his cheekbone. A.J. couldn't tell if it was from his lip or his nose. Lavalle wasn't smiling any-

more, but he was still standing. Landau had intervened too
soon.

The coach grabbed the boy's attention again by poking
at his chest with a thick finger.

"You want to play the tough guy, you do it out there.
In here, you belong to *me*. And I don't give second chances
for that garbage," Landau snarled. "You're gone, mister.
Five games. I don't want to see your face for a month.
Maybe not even then."

A sound from Lavalle, the start of a word. Landau
whipped around, slicing it off.

"Don't you even open your smart-ass mouth," he ordered. "You're walking a thin line with me, Lavalle. You
push it and I swear, you're next."

The referee's whistle shrieked, cutting the heavy air. It
was the signal to start the third period. No one moved.

Landau glowered at them. "Well, shake it! Hustle! You
want me to suspend the bloody lot of you?"

They started to file out, the rumble of disbelief like a
tremor among them. Lavalle was wiping his face with his
sleeve as he trudged past. He didn't even look in A.J.'s
direction.

Weitzammer grabbed A.J.'s arm. "Hey," he said quietly.
"I'll talk to Landau. We'll get you back real soon." A
pause. "I don't know what happened, but . . . but
Lavalle probably asked for it. He's a jerk, A.J."

A.J. was staring at the lockers, where Lavalle had been.
Weitzammer could hardly hear him breathing.

The captain gave A.J.'s arm a friendly shake. "Hang in
there," he said, before he turned and left.

A.J. counted to a hundred. Then he stripped and showered. He was under the water a long time. He washed his hair twice, maybe three times; he lost track.

The empty locker room felt haunted. Noise from the game seeped in, eerily distorted, as if there were a rip in the wall and somebody else's life was leaking into his. He didn't stay long enough to shave.

A.J. walked outside and sat down in the snow.

Christmas was coming. The lights on the houses seemed to swell and contract, as if they were breathing.

A.J., get up. You're sitting in the snow.

But it couldn't be Christmas yet. They hadn't gotten a tree or anything. And he hadn't done his shopping. He always left it until the end, anyway. He never knew what to get people.

Your ass is freezing, A.J., get up!

Last year they'd gotten a surprise, him and his dad. The day before Christmas a lady had shown up at their door, holding a basket of fruit, all wrapped up in red cellophane. She was from their church, she'd said, and they'd had a special bazaar to raise money for gifts for single parents. She'd handed over the basket as if it were holy myrrh. When the door was closed, he and his dad had stared at each other, then burst out laughing. They'd never gone to church.

You idiot. You can't sit here all night. Summer's on her way to meet you.

A.J. lurched to his feet, pain shooting through his legs and backside. He couldn't face her with the arena emptying and the team spilling out into the night. Summer would know, sooner or later, but he couldn't bear for it to be tonight.

And he had to get her to Treejack's. They had to be
there together. He began to run.

The wind blew his hair into his eyes. If he was cold, he
didn't feel it. He didn't pause, he didn't slow down. He felt
like a piece of machinery, a metal man, that once set into
motion, was powerless to stop.

He startled her.

"What are you doing here?" Summer cried, when she
opened the door to him panting on the step.

A.J. leaned against the doorframe on his forearm. He
couldn't ever remember running like that.

"What's the matter?" Summer asked. "Did the game
end early? Is something wrong? Where's Tully? I thought
you wanted me to meet you at the arena."

A.J. shrugged. Then he lifted his head and looked at
her.

Summer was not the type of girl who fussed. She did
not spend half a date in the bathroom, fixing. To A.J. it
was the way she moved, the way she held her head, that
was the sparkle of her.

Tonight was different. Tonight she had fussed, a little.
Being a boy, he couldn't tell what she had done exactly.
All he knew was that the sight of her split him open.
Powder-blue clothes, the color of blue jeans after you've
washed and worn them forever. The subtlest shine of pink
around her mouth, a dot of gold on each earlobe. And
something else. A softness seemed to surround her, powdery and perfect, as if she had been dusted all over with
icing sugar.

"A.J.?" Summer said.

"Can we go now?" he asked abruptly.

Summer sighed. "Sure, why not. Come in while I get my coat."

But he waited on the porch, hands jammed into his pockets, feeling the warm air waft through the open door. Summer looked at him strangely as she stepped out, but by that time he was already heading for the sidewalk.

They were halfway to Treejack's before she asked.

"Why are we walking so fast? What's the hurry?"

"Sorry," A.J. said, slowing down, eyes glued to the ground.

For a few minutes there was only the muted padding of their footsteps.

"A.J., what's wrong?" Summer asked finally.

"Nothing."

"Did you have a bad game?"

"I thought you never wanted to hear about *the game.*" Immediately he was sorry. None of this was her fault. Fumbling, shy, he reached for her hand, but it was in her pocket. There were a few awkward moments before she realized what he wanted. Then they walked the rest of the way, mittens clenched, to Treejack's house.

It was a zoo. Someone had written, "Parents in Florida —come on in" in spray-snow on the big picture window. Every light was blazing and the music thumped like a reckless heart. They could feel its raw beat on the walkway. Through the windows they could see the kids inside pressed shoulder to shoulder, a twisting, writhing mob. Summer's mitten squeezed his. A.J. squeezed back.

They welcomed him like a hero. It was too loud to actually hear anything, but they slapped him on the back and gestured. Hotshot. Bad Boy. A.J.'s polite smile felt painted on. What if they all knew? he wondered. How welcome would he be then?

He led Summer into the kitchen, hoping there would be fewer people in there. But if anything, the kitchen was worse. It was where the liquor flowed from. Kids were sitting on the counters as well as filling the small, sticky floor space. Normally this would have panicked him, the touching, pushing and pressing, but tonight was different. He moved through the throng feeling numb, as if he were still sitting in the snow.

Treejack was in the kitchen. But he was too drunk to be dangerous, A.J. realized. *His* party had started at five in the afternoon. Treejack scoured Summer with a long, leering look, then gave A.J. the "thumbs up" sign behind her back.

"How ya doing?" he cried over the noise.

"Fine!" Summer shouted back.

"How's your brother? He coming tonight?"

"No! He's at the Elks!" Summer shouted.

There was a big Christmas party every year at the Elks hall. It was supposed to be a great time if you could get tickets. A.J. was glad that Tully had. Beneath his numb shell, some instinct told him that there wasn't room in this sweaty, swarming house for both of them tonight.

Before he left the kitchen, Treejack dragged A.J. over beside the refrigerator.

"It's all yours if you want it," he said, jerking his head towards a door near the back entrance. He pulled out a key that he pressed, grinning, into A.J.'s hand. A key for a *basement*? A.J. wondered.

"It used to be a suite," Treejack explained, and then he giggled. A.J. stared. Treejack had had more than just liquor tonight.

"Have a ball," Treejack said. He burst into laughter. "Get it? Get it?" He wandered away, still giggling.

A.J. put the key in his front jeans pocket. It lay so flat no one would have known it was there.

· SIXTEEN ·

"ALL RIGHT, WHO is she?" Summer asked pointedly.

"What?" A.J. looked up.

"I thought that would wake you," Summer sighed. "You've been totally hypnotized by something—or someone—since we got here. I try to talk to you and you stare off into space!"

"Sorry. I couldn't hear you," he mumbled. "The music's too loud." Just as he said it, he realized that the music *wasn't* loud, that somehow it had faded to a comfortable buzz in the background. The crowd, too, had thinned, although most of the rowdies were still there.

A.J. glanced surreptitiously at his watch. 11:30! Almost two hours had evaporated into the air, and he didn't know how.

"Look, it's not that I care," Summer continued, her arms folded over her chest. "Be with whoever you want. But you invited me, remember? These are your friends. Bored and ignored I can get at home."

They were in a hallway, near a linen closet. A.J. couldn't remember how they'd got here, or why, but for the moment they were alone. He put his hands on her shoulders, maybe too quickly. She flinched.

"There's nobody," he said. "I . . . I'm just not with it tonight. Really, there's nobody. I've liked you for so long," he whispered.

He knew he was looking at her too intently. Summer's eyes were wide and her mouth was drawn into a small pink line. His insides were racing. He had somehow surged into third gear, without ever hitting first or second.

"A.J., is something wrong?" she asked again. "Is there something you want to talk about?"

My whole freaking life is wrong, he thought. He felt pressed up against a creaking, groaning dam, scrambling to plug the leaks, not knowing which ones were biggest or worst, just jumping to cover this hole, and the next and the next.

"There's a place where we can talk," he said.

She did not see him use the key. He hunched in front of the door and pretended the knob was sticking. She balked at going down the stairs, but he took her hand, no mittens this time, and gently, firmly, guided her into the dark.

He didn't turn on the light. The two high basement windows faced the street, and once their eyes adjusted, they could make out the small fridge and table and couch. Summer turned around. Her powder-blue clothes had faded to noncolor. A.J. shivered. *All cats are gray in the dark.*

"Now," she said. "What is it?"

He kissed her. "A.J.!" she giggled. He kissed her again, and again. He was not particularly good at it—he hadn't had much opportunity for practice—but he liked her, and he understood about hugging. Pretty soon she was kissing him back.

He steered her towards the couch and eased them both onto it. He wondered at his own courage; last August he could hardly look her in the eye. But the whole world had changed since August.

He nuzzled her neck, inhaling the scent of her hair. She made a soft sound, but it was not an unhappy sound, and that was good.

Except nothing was happening. A.J. felt the sudden pitch of panic. He was holding her and kissing her, and nothing! These last few weeks he'd been overwhelmed by his own heat. There couldn't be nothing now!

He held her tightly so that she would know how strong he was. When he kissed her, he could feel her neck muscles strain. She was struggling to keep her head upright. There were little noises, the rustle of clothing, murmurs in her throat; they sounded far away. He was caught up in his own sound, his breath like a train in her hair.

Oh, yes. Oh, yes, I can. He played the words over and over in his head, a chant to kindle the tiny fire that had finally leapt into being.

He was burning her now. She turned away from his mouth, trying to avoid the sandpaper stubble of his chin. He didn't care. He found her collar and burrowed in against the soft skin of her neck.

Do you get the message, Tulsa Brown? his heart cried.

Summer tried to say something; A.J. wasn't listening. He wanted to press an imprint of himself on her, on her skin. This was how it was supposed to be. His hands knew the way without being told.

"A.J., don't."

They were such little words, almost inaudible. He let them flutter away.

"Come on, I mean it."

But she didn't; she couldn't. When she pushed at him with her hand, it felt like a bird's wing. He was so strong. Metal man.

"A.J.! God damn you—stop!"

He didn't know how it happened, how she wrenched herself out of his grip. One moment she was pressed against him and the next she was on her feet, trembling in the silver light.

"Who do you think you are?" she whispered. A tear sprang over her eyelashes. She wiped at it angrily.

"Who do you think you are!" Louder this time, shriller. The noise alarmed him. He moved to get up, moved his lips to say, "Shh." She leapt back, as if yanked by a string.

"Don't you come near me." She was struggling to button her blouse, but her hands were shaking, and she would not take her eyes off him. "I swear to God I'll scream."

The tears were sliding one after another now, too fast and too many to brush away. She wasn't supposed to cry. A.J. took a step, reaching out to touch her arm.

"Summer," he started.

She turned and bolted for the stairs.

In the empty kitchen, Tully was just opening his first beer. He hadn't expected the party to have wound down yet; Treejack was notorious for his all-nighters. But considering the wasted look of the half-dozen people left, Tully wasn't surprised that the party was dying.

When the basement door burst open, he jerked up his head. Brother and sister stared at each other. He grasped the details in one sickening clutch, like catching a razor blade with his hand. Her tangled hair and twisted clothes; the dark mascara tracks on her pretty, proud face.

Tully set his beer on the counter. Summer turned to dash for the front door. He caught her by the shoulders.

"What the . . . ?"

A sob shook her, but she would not look at him. She twisted away, intent on getting her coat and getting out. For a single stunned moment Tully watched her go. Then he whirled around and lunged for the basement, thundering down the stairs.

"I don't know who the hell you are, but you've got a real problem now, scum," Tully spat into the darkness.

Lit by the open door above, he was a blaze in the cold basement. Arms rigid, fists tight, blond hair wild and white, like sparks around his head.

Standing near the wall, far from the light, A.J. stared. He could hardly breathe. He was utterly locked into this voyeur's fantasy, the dark thrill of seeing without being seen. The thought throbbed in him like a pulse. *I could break you. I could break you into pieces, you stupid queer bastard.*

"You picked the wrong girl to jerk around. That was my sister, scum!" Tully hammered the particleboard wall. "That's a real big fucking problem!"

A.J. could see him so clearly, his heaving chest and corded muscles, even the gleam of sweat at his throat. *I have only one problem, Tulsa Brown. You are my problem. And I'm going to fix it right now.*

"Come and get me, faggot," he said.

Tully's head jerked towards the noise, his lips parted in

disbelief. Then he swore, a cry of rage and despair, and charged blindly at the far wall.

A.J. leaned into the slam with his big shoulder, and sent Tully staggering backwards, clattering hard into some shelves. It was a solid, satisfying check and A.J. leapt forward to finish it.

But he had forgotten how quick Tully was, how strong he was. A forearm snapped A.J.'s head back in a painful explosion. He reeled into a chair, gouging himself. But when Tully grabbed for him, he grabbed, too, and they flipped and stumbled and swung and dragged each other up until . . . until . . .

A.J.'s arm was wrenched behind his back, the socket screaming. The textured wall dug into the side of his face.

"Is that it?" Tully hissed into his ear. He shoved again, harder. "Is that everything?" A.J. clenched his teeth to keep from crying out. He nodded. Tully pushed himself away.

A.J. slumped heavily against the wall, his breath like a furnace on his face.

Tully walked a few steps, swaying. When he got to the windows, he leaned on the ledge, which came up under his armpit. Then he put his hand over his face.

A.J. closed his eyes. He'd gotten stitches once, when he was eight. Tobogganing down a hill, he'd slid into a barbed wire fence, tearing his pants and gashing himself. One of the kids screamed and the other one started to cry, there was so much blood. But it didn't hurt.

His dad had rushed him to the hospital, the leg wrapped in ice. The doctor had shot him full of Novocain and put in thirty-two stitches, while A.J. watched in fascinated silence. It still didn't hurt.

Then A.J. had gone to sleep. And in the night the freezing wore off and the shock wore off and he'd woken up, doubled over and shaking in his bed.

This was exactly like that.

"Don't go near my family," Tully said through his hand. "Don't go near my house." His voice quavered and he stopped, before it broke.

A.J.'s throat was on fire. It was supposed to be better now, right? He had settled himself with Lavalle and proved himself to Treejack and given Tully the message, even though he'd lost. But it wasn't any better.

"I'll never forgive you," A.J. said thickly.

Tully kicked at the wall and spun around, green eyes glittering.

"There's nothing to forgive! Why can't you get that through your head? I don't need your permission, A.J. How I live and who I love has got nothing to do with you."

Permission. The word snaked inside A.J.'s head.

Tully turned away again, disgusted. A.J. could not keep himself from staring at the boy's back. Half of Tully's shirt had come untucked, and one shoulder seam had ripped.

"I never did that to you," Tully said, his breath touching the glass. "When you were fighting so bad with your dad, I never said you should do this, or that. You were my friend. I liked you. I really liked you."

There was only the two of them, barely six feet from shoulder to shoulder. The big room was suddenly as close and familiar as the front seat of the Mustang.

"When did you know, Tul?" A.J. blurted.

"Know what?" Tully said tiredly.

"When did you know? *How* did you know?"

Tully looked up. A.J. hadn't moved. He was still a

shadow huddled against a dark wall. But Tully's eyes had adjusted now, and he could see the outline of A.J. clearly. So big. So handsome. So scared.

"I was seven," Tully started quietly. "I know I was seven because that was the year I got my red two-wheeler. You know, the one in the garage?"

A.J. nodded, not understanding what this had to do with anything.

"I was sitting on my bike near the gate in the back-yard," Tully continued. "It had to be a Saturday because Mom and Dad were both home. They were standing in front of the garden, not looking at me, just talking about what they were going to put in that year. It was like a photograph somehow, Mom and Dad and the house and the garden, all pressed into this picture. And sitting there on my bike, I just knew that I didn't fit there. It wasn't ever going to be my picture, not even when I grew up."

A.J. was stunned. Seven. This wasn't what he'd expected. This didn't have anything to do with sex.

"Was . . . was there ever a person," he stammered, his mouth dry. "Was there ever somebody . . . that . . . that started it?"

Tully snorted. "I'm not going to recount my entire adolescence, if you don't mind. Of course there was somebody."

"How did you know that was *it?* How did you know that it wasn't just maybe that one person you liked who . . . who . . ." A.J. broke off, choking.

Tully took a step closer. "A.J., what are you trying to say?"

A.J. closed his eyes. God damn him. God damn him for not knowing.

"Everybody wants you, Tully." He rushed the words out, trembling. "Can't you see that? Everybody loves you and everybody wants you, even if they can't, even if they shouldn't."

The realization settled on Tully like snow. "Even you?" he said.

"Yes," A.J. whispered. A car rumbled past in the street, a small vibration in the floor and walls.

"I've always wanted you," Tully said quietly, finally.

A.J. did not speak. There was a hurricane roaring inside his ears. His heart was thudding so hard he was afraid he would black out. The night had stopped.

He ran his hands over his face. How had this awful moment ever gotten into his life? I'm just a regular guy, A.J. thought numbly. I play hockey. I go to school. I live in this crummy little city in the middle of nowhere. I'm just so freaking regular. Except I want to die.

A.J. folded his arms over his chest and stared at the floor. "I'm scared, Tul," he said. "This can't be happening—but I don't know how to stop it. What are we going to do?"

Tully was dizzy. It was like he was standing at the edge of a precipice, and even though he was so high, every detail was sharp, exhilaratingly clear. He could hardly believe this opportunity was in front of him, the one he had never dared wish for, the one he could throw his heart into. The very rush of air urged him over, pulled at him like a magnet.

And he knew it was wrong. Knowing A.J., knowing himself, it was completely wrong. This time Tully took a breath and stepped back, away from the edge.

"Nothing," he said. "We're going to do nothing."

A.J. wondered if he'd heard right.

Tully leaned back against the wall that had the window. "Look," he said. "It's no big deal to have a crush on somebody. Everybody has crushes. But there's a big difference between having a crush and being gay."

"What's the difference?" A.J. asked softly.

"How do you explain the color red to somebody who's never seen it?" Tully wondered aloud. "Jesus, I don't know."

But the silence told him he had to explain it, that it mattered very much. Tully tried again. "I know what you're thinking, what you're worrying about. But don't. If you were gay you'd know by now. You don't turn twenty-one and wake up one morning to find a note from God on your pillow." A pause. "This is me, but it isn't you, A.J. As real and as scary as it seems right now, for you it's going to go away. Not today, not tomorrow, but pretty soon. And that day we'll both be glad that we didn't let anything happen."

A.J. finally had the courage to lift his eyes, and he was overwhelmed. He thought he knew that face, but this man's profile cut into the window light, he hardly knew at all.

When had it happened? the boy wondered. How had Tully grown up in less than a season, less than a semester? When had he learned such control?

A.J. felt small and sick and alone. A corner of his heart resented that Tully wasn't going to be alone, even with Derek Lavalle out of the picture. There would be somebody new because there always was. Tully was one of those people other people loved.

"They're going to find out someday," A.J. said, meaning

the whole world but thinking of Treejack and Doerkson. "They're going to find out and it's going to be rough."

"Hey, I'm Prince Charming, remember?" Tully said, bitterness sharpening the words. "There's only six months before grad, anyway. School's the worst."

School. That reality jogged A.J. He pushed himself off the wall. He started walking around to restore his circulation, moving his shoulder gingerly.

"I think you broke my freaking arm," he said.

"That's nothing compared to what Summer's going to do."

A.J. stopped. The memory of her snapped open inside him like a switchblade. For an instant he saw her vividly, backing away from him, her hands clutching her shirt.

"I have to see her," A.J. blurted. "Right now."

"What? Are you nuts? It's after one o'clock," Tully said.

A.J. wavered. Maybe he should just let it go, for now. He could call tomorrow. Or sometime. Or . . .

He shook the thought off and took a breath. "Tonight, Tul. I scared her, and I . . . I hurt her, and I don't know what the hell I'm going to say, but it's got to be tonight."

Tully just looked at him. A.J. couldn't guess what was going on behind those green eyes. Finally he smiled, a little grimly. "I've got something to tell her, too," he said. "Let's go."

They moved silently across the floor, heading for the stairway. But halfway up the stairs, A.J. hesitated. Tully almost stepped up into him, then backed down.

"What?" he said.

A.J. stared straight ahead. "I know what you said about you and me not being the same, Tul. But I can't risk it. I can't ever have the chance to know, for sure."

"No," Tully promised. "Never."

A.J. swallowed. "I've got to have my weights back. In my house. Tonight."

It was a wounded silence. A.J. knew Tully didn't believe how necessary this was. But after a moment the other boy said, "Sure. Whatever you want." Tully reached up and thunked A.J. solidly on the back. "Let's go," he said again. And they walked up into the light.

• SEVENTEEN •

AND SO A.J. started lifting again. When he set up the weights in his room, he was surprised by how inconsequential they looked—just the small bench and slender bar; the innocuous plates and bells. In his head the past few months, they had seemed much, much bigger.

He woke up looking at them and went to sleep too tired to dream. "Every time you drop one of those things, I think somebody keeled over," June said, but the weights filled the gap. And in the longest, coldest months of the prairie winter, there were a lot of gaps. A.J. had found out what Tully already knew. When Summer got mad, she stayed mad.

Facing her that night had been punishment in itself. Stammering, shy, he'd told her about the fight with Lavalle, and getting suspended from the team, and Treejack.

"So you were feeling threatened and stressed," Summer analyzed in her merciless way. "You think that makes you something special? Welcome to the human race, He-man. Everybody has troubles, but that doesn't entitle them to attack people. You would have thought of that—if you ever thought of anything except yourself."

She cut and cut, and he sat, his hands clasped, bleeding silently. But he had to let her settle the score her way.

"I hope you didn't come here to apologize," she finished flatly, "because if you did, I don't accept it."

Tully's story she accepted, so calmly and so quickly A.J. was bewildered. There was something about families—or girls, or Summer—that defied him. It was almost as if she'd known, as if she'd been expecting this.

A.J. had not expected it. Listening to Tully made him break into a cold sweat. Summer just said, "Oh, Tulsa." Then she launched into a drill about safe sex, so detailed and knowledgeable that Tully rolled his eyes, and A.J. blushed into third-degree burns.

January was a cold month. A.J. divided his time between home—the weights—and school. Doerkson and Rasmussen, even Treejack, pestered him to hang around. Word about his spectacular goal had gotten out. It was almost as though his suspension didn't count, or that it somehow added to the mystique. Bad Boy, A.J. thought, shaking his head. He shrugged their invitations off.

He went to the outdoor rink late in the evenings, when it was too cold and too dark to be crowded. He skated endless laps, and ran relentlessly through the drills he hated, letting the pain and exhaustion soak him like rain.

This is how you're safe, the boy thought, racing under the moon. This is how you'll be sane.

That didn't keep him from knocking on Landau's door the first day of February. The verbal whipping was everything he'd expected, and more. A.J. felt the objections rising up his esophagus like breakfast, but he clamped his mouth shut. Landau, like Summer, had the right to his shot.

Eventually the coach ran out of steam, and relented. "But don't go getting cocky," he warned. "You're on probation, mister. You're marginal."

So what else is new? A.J. thought.

It was after one of his first practices, when he was just starting to feel settled again and thinking that his plan was working, that Tully wandered by the sink while A.J. was shaving. "Hey, you want a ride home?" he said.

A.J. almost cut himself. "Nah, it's okay. I can walk," he said casually.

Tully was hanging on to both ends of a towel around his neck. "It's about Summer," he said quietly. "I've got to talk to you."

The hook reeled him in. In a few minutes A.J. found himself sitting on the passenger side of the Mustang, a place he'd sworn he'd never be again. The rush of nostalgia caught him by surprise—the familiar buttons and dials, the smooth leather seat that was so easy to slide into.

A.J. tried not to show it. He stared out the windshield and asked, "So what's the trouble with Summer?"

"She's in a bad way," Tully said seriously. "She's pining for you."

A.J. almost laughed out loud. "Get real! She hates me."

"No, no, I mean it! She mopes around, she can't sleep. The girl is lovesick."

A.J. snorted. "She's probably preoccupied planning my crucifixion." This time Tully laughed.

"Well, she *has* had a few estimates done. . . . You've

got no idea what a good old-fashioned execution costs these days. Whips, cross, thorns—it all adds up. I tell you," Tully continued, "when my sister wastes somebody, she does it *right.*"

A.J. started to giggle. He couldn't help it.

"And since she's going to such trouble," Tully said, "since she's going to such *expense,* there's no need for you to do it yourself."

A.J.'s grin tightened and shifted. Goal. Unassisted. On a fake shot. You never miss, do you, Tul? A.J. thought. You've got the angles down pat. But in his chest, the amazement was running through him like an underground spring. How did Tully know him so well?

They drove quietly through the snowy streets. When they pulled up to A.J.'s house, Tully said, "I didn't lie."

"About what?"

"About Summer. She wouldn't make this much noise if you weren't important."

"Oh, sure."

"Anyhow, I think you should give the kid a break. Thrill her with your presence. Come over and hang around. Even my parents wonder about you. They keep asking why we've got so much food in the house these days." Tully paused. "Everybody misses you, A.J. And there's no future in being a hermit. No salary, no benefits."

One side of A.J.'s mouth curled ruefully. "Yeah, but at least I have job security." He got out of the car.

"See you!" Tully called out his window. A.J. felt a small gust of warmth, like the barest breath of spring, and his hand leapt up in a wave. But then he caught himself. This wasn't part of the plan. He had it all mapped out in his head, what he had to do and the way it had to be, to be safe.

A.J. stood, watching the snub back end of the Mustang as it roared down the street. Nothing personal, Tul, he thought. Live your life however you want. But don't expect me to be part of it.

He went inside and up to his room and in a few minutes he was under 150 pounds, trying to push it through the ceiling. But he couldn't help remembering how the laughter had felt in his throat.

In March he received an invitation to his second cousin Georgette's wedding. The envelope was addressed to Mr. A. Brandiosa. It shocked him to think he was a Mr. to anybody.

He read over the embossed script on parchment, then tossed it carelessly on the table. His father picked it up.

"Are you going to go?" Decco asked.

A.J. shrugged. "I don't know. Probably not."

"Why not?"

A.J. felt an uncomfortable tightening under his rib cage. He pictured himself in the crowded dance hall with all those strangers, or worse, family. He could see himself standing miserably against the wall, alone.

"I don't have . . ."

"A date?" June asked, walking into the room.

A.J. colored from his neck to his hairline. "No. A decent suit. I don't think my old one fits."

"Try it," Decco said.

A.J. tried, grumbling, self-conscious. When he reached down to uncurl his pant leg, he snapped the shoulders out of the jacket.

"I don't believe it," Decco said, circling him, surveying the broken seams. "Look at you."

"Yeah, look at me." The boy was grinning with amazement. "Now I *really* don't have a suit," he said. "I guess I can't go."

"Well, isn't grad coming up, too?" June asked. The woman clung like a barnacle, A.J. thought. How could she be thinking ahead to *his* grad when even he wasn't?

"Maybe we should go look around," Decco said.

That Saturday A.J. found himself in the unusual circumstance of being out with his father. He stared at the passing scenery, not knowing what to talk about. It was rare for them to be alone these days.

"This is where I go," Decco said, pulling into a parking lot. "It's a good store."

It *was* a good store, with silver-haired clerks in shiny shoes, and razor-sharp pleats in their flannel pants. There was no music in the background, only the distant hum of a sewing machine.

A.J. tried on six suits, including a charcoal gray that made him look so tall and so dark, it startled him.

"I think it needs a little shaping," the clerk said, and with a few pins he nipped in the waist of the jacket so that it followed the boy's big frame perfectly.

"What do you think?" Decco asked when the clerk had courteously left them alone.

A.J. couldn't take his eyes off the image of the man in the mirror. Mr. A. Brandiosa. "It's . . . it's really great," he said. Then he felt a guilty pang. "It's too good, just for grad. I could rent a tux or something."

Decco was leaning against a pillar, his arms folded over

his chest. A.J. could just catch him, behind his own image, in the mirror's reflection.

"I think you should go to this wedding, A.J.," he said quietly. "It would be good for you. You don't go out much anymore. I don't see your friends around the house. Maybe it's none of my business, but you seem to be working so hard at something. Too hard."

Decco turned his head, shifted his gaze to another wall, another rack of suits. "Don't get me wrong. It's good to fix your sights on something and then run after it. But you can run so far and so long by yourself that the day comes when you realize you don't know how to be with people anymore. You want somebody and you need somebody but you don't even know what it's supposed to be like."

The heat took A.J. by surprise—a sudden welling in his throat and eyes. It was as unexpected as this store, this day.

He took off the suit carefully in the dressing room, trying not to pull out the tailor's pins. He put on his own clothes slowly, giving himself time to settle. And he walked back out into the fluorescent light, knowing that he would try to be better, try to be nicer to the woman who was sitting and waiting for his father.

The night of the wedding A.J. felt light and clear-headed. He was still shy walking in alone, but the suit helped a lot. The maid of honor gave him a kiss *and* a wink.

Then, "Holy mother! You rob a bank or what?"

A.J.'s head jerked up and all the muscles in his back and shoulders curled. Tully. The blond boy was wearing a periwinkle-blue suit jacket, probably the only one in Moose Jaw. The sleeves were pushed up to the elbow, and he had on his dark sunglasses, of course.

He lifted them to get a better look at A.J.'s suit. "Let me guess. You've got rich family you never told me about."

A.J. stepped back, self-conscious. He tried to change the subject. "Speaking of family," he said, nodding towards the bride and groom, "don't tell me we're related."

"God, no. Unless you can be related through a babysitter. I used to give Georgette nervous breakdowns when I was five."

A.J. grinned. He believed that somehow. Tully leaned against the wall.

"How've you been?" he asked.

"Fine," A.J. said, but he couldn't make it sound natural, couldn't make it sound like the truth. For a moment there was only the music, country crossover, and the general noise of human beings. Then Tully turned and pushed up his sunglasses again.

"Come sit at our table," he said. "Okay? Please?"

His eyes were naked. A.J. could read them perfectly. They were full of reassurance, full of the promise he'd made in Treejack's basement. No. Never. Don't worry.

After all this, A.J. thought, and he still won't give up. After all this, and he still wants to be my friend.

But he only shrugged. "Sure, what the hell. I don't have anywhere else to sit." He followed the buoyant blue jacket to a table near the dance floor.

"You didn't!" Summer screeched when she saw him. "You didn't bring Attila the Hun *here*. The mad slasher, the depraved defense—"

A.J. took a deep breath and pulled up a chair right beside her.

"I know you love it, but try and control yourself, all right?" he said boldly. The half-dozen people at the table burst into laughter. Summer's jaw dropped, but then she snapped it shut. Her cheeks were pink for a long time.

A.J. could feel the knots in his shoulders uncurling. So he wasn't being nice. But neither was she. You could only say you were sorry for so long. He'd probably bruised her ego, but didn't he have feelings, too? How come—

"Well, are you going to leave me sitting here all night?" Summer said suddenly. "Civilized people ask other civilized people to dance, you know."

As A.J. stood up, Tully caught his eye and winked.

A.J. danced with Summer, and then again later, and then again even later, slow. She didn't get too close, but close enough. He was afraid his sweaty hand would leave a mark on the waist of her dress. She leaned forward once, to whisper in his ear, and he was so surprised he almost stepped on her.

"That's a nice suit," Summer said.

It was, A.J. thought, the warmth easing through him. It was a nice suit, and a nice night. He wondered how his father had known.

A few minutes later, everything changed. As A.J. was walking back from the bar with a glass of beer in each hand, he heard a cry behind him.

"Hey, A.J.!"

Uncle Mike. A.J. cringed. He kept walking, pretending he hadn't heard.

"You . . . A.J.!" the old man roared. People looked up. A.J. finally stopped, wishing he could crawl under a table. He managed a grudging smile as Uncle Mike wheezed up alongside him.

The old man hung on his arm, catching his breath. "Jeez

. . . what's with . . . you? You think you had the puck
or something?"

Uncle Mike walloped him on the back, delighted with
his own cleverness. A.J. had to lurch to keep the glasses
from spilling.

"So, that team of yours is going to the finals this year?"
Mike asked.

"Yeah, it looks like it. The season's not over yet,
though."

Mike's eyebrows gathered in disapproval. "You gotta do
your part, you know. I don't see your name in the paper
much anymore."

You mean I haven't beat anybody up lately, the boy
thought.

"Bad time to go losing your spunk," Mike said omi-
nously. "It's those gol-darned pansy coaches—hold a kid
back."

A.J. shifted irritably.

Uncle Mike paused to light one of his foul cigars. "I see
your dad's not here tonight," he said, shaking out the
match.

The back of A.J.'s neck prickled.

"No, he's not," he said stiffly.

"I hear he's kinda busy these days. Got himself a new
girl." Mike's mouth wrapped around the word. He made
it sound unsavory. "Don't get me wrong, kid," he said in a
hushed voice. "It's nothing personal. Hell, every man's en-
titled to his own life. But if you ask me . . ."

Nothing personal. A.J. knew the weight of those words,
the shape of them, and how they'd sounded inside his own
head.

Oh, God, he thought. Not this. Not this narrow, obnoxious old man. Not me. But the familiarity was choking
him. It filled his throat and nose, as odorous as Mike's
cigar.

Mike tried to drape his arm across the boy's big shoulders. ". . . and people are going to talk," he was saying.
"Now, I'm all for this freedom thing, and I love your
dad—"

A.J. shook him off. "No, you don't," he said hoarsely.
"You don't love him at all. Because if you did . . ."

He didn't say it. He turned and strode away, leaving
Uncle Mike to stare after him, mouth open. A.J. knew he'd
get the "respect your elders" lecture tomorrow, but he
didn't care. Some elders didn't deserve respect.

He was so grateful to get to his table. It was near the
dance floor so the music was louder. When he set a glass in
front of Summer, she squeezed his arm quickly. Then she
turned her attention back to the floor, to where Tully was
dancing with a bridesmaid.

It was hard not to watch Tully. The spotlights lit up his
wild blue jacket and glanced off the obsidian surface of his
glasses. He was air-guitaring, the electric lead for that eter-
nal rock group in his head. The bridesmaid watched him in
adoration. Other people just watched, eyebrows raised. He
was a siren.

A.J. leaned forward, resting his arm on the back of Summer's chair. When his warm hand curled around her bare
shoulder, she didn't pull away.

A.J. knew he would never air-guitar, but he couldn't
help admiring what he saw. To be trapped in this room
with people like Uncle Mike—people like *me,* A.J.

thought with a pang—and to dance anyway, dance in joy, took an especially resilient human being.

Keep on dancing, Tul, A.J. thought, and he gave Summer's shoulder a squeeze.

· ABOUT THE AUTHOR ·

DIANA WIELER LIVES with her husband and son in Winnipeg, Manitoba, Canada. She is the author of *Last Chance Summer.*